Barnsley Libraries

CENTRA

P.S.2027

Ret

29. JUL 19.

3805970006261 7

NO MAN'S LAND

The Captain Riley Adventures

BY

FERNANDO GAMBOA

First Digital Edition: September, 2017
First Printed Edition: September, 2017

© Fernando Gamboa, 2017
All rights reserved. No part of this book may be reproduced or transmitted in any form or by any means without the written permission of the author, including reproductions intended for renting or public lending.
www.gamboabooks.com

Original Title: *Tierra de nadie*
Translated from the Spanish by Christy Cox and Peter Gauld
Edited by Carmen Grau

... this country is far too beautiful for the Fascists to have it. They have already made Germany and Italy and Austria so loathsome that even the scenery is inadequate, and every time I drive on the roads here and see the rock mountains and the tough terraced fields, and the umbrella pines above the beaches, and the dust colored villages and the gravel river beds and the peasants' faces, I think: Save Spain for the decent people, it's too beautiful to waste.

Letter from Martha Gellhorn to Eleanor Roosevelt
1938

1

August 24, 1937

26 miles south-east of Zaragoza, Spain

    That noon at the end of August 1937, the sun beat down like a biblical curse on the five hundred men of the Lincoln Brigade who were marching along the narrow dirt path, forming a more or less homogenous column that stretched out for nearly a quarter of a mile. Each of them was carrying a Mauser rifle, a blanket and a bundle with a tin plate and mug, ammunition in their belts and a couple of changes of underwear, as dirty and worn out as what they had on. They were covered with the fine yellow dust of those lands and looked like some tired parade of living dead who had come out for a stroll.

    The hypnotic buzzing of the cicadas overlapped with the rough background noise of a thousand boots dragging themselves along. Wherever they looked, fields of olives and dried-up land, abandoned because of the war, stretched to the horizon. Behind them the smoking bell tower of the village of Quinto had disappeared into the distance hours before. It had been taken barely the day before by those same men, at too high a price. Ahead, outlined against a washed-out blue sky, was the dark silhouette, low and elongated, of the place which was their true destination: Belchite.

Lieutenant Alexander M. Riley walked at the head of the First Company. His dirty, untidy black hair fell over his forehead almost to his amber eyes, which were half-closed until they were little more than two grooves framed by the thick beard covering his wide jaw that he had not been able to shave in two weeks. His shirt, which long ago had been white, stuck to his body like a stinking second skin, his worn-out flannel trousers felt like esparto grass, his old boots barely rose from the ground at each step, and the Colt pistol he carried in his belt felt as though it was loaded with a mortar.

Alex Riley moved on with the tired step of one who has been marching since dawn under an infernal heat, but forced himself to appear lively so as to not show weakness before the soldiers who were with him as a small advance group. In it, among many others, were Sergeants Vernon Shelby (a West Point student who had not finished his course), John G. Honeycombe (a member of the Californian Communist Party), Harry Fisher (an Ohio architect, just graduated) and Joaquín Alcántara, a rotund Galician cook who had settled in Brooklyn and a loyal friend of Alex's since the beginning of the war whose life he had saved during the tragic assault on the Pingarrón six months earlier.

At that moment, raising a cloud of dust as he came, Commander Robert Merriman caught up with them on a dapple-grey horse. Tugging at the reins, he brought the animal to a stop beside them, jumped down nimbly and came to stand before Riley.

The former professor of Economics at the University of California and currently commander of that brigade which consisted only of volunteers from the United States, was an intelligent and resolute man. Good-looking, he was as tall as Riley and whatever the occasion sported an impeccable peaked cap, commander's jacket and knee-high boots which seemed immune to the sticky dust of the Spanish fields. "How's everything going around here, Alex?" he asked bluntly as he took him aside.

"Quite well," he replied. After a brief glance at his men he added, "Although I think this would be a good time to rest and get our strength back in the shade of those olive trees. The men are exhausted."

Merriman looked around, squinting behind his spectacles. "Seems a good idea. We'll camp here and wait for orders. And make sure they dig a few sniper trenches at the edge of the olive grove. I don't want any surprises."

"Right, sir," he replied, and leaning a little closer he asked him in a low voice: "Have they told you when they're planning the assault?"

Merriman's face twitched. "Who knows, Alex," he said in the same tone, so that the men would not hear. "I wish it was never. You know I believe that attacking this darn village is complete insanity that'll cost us time and lives, but in the War Ministry they insist we do it, and nobody's been able to convince Indalecio Prieto otherwise. So…" He left the sentence unfinished and shrugged.

Riley clicked his tongue in displeasure. "I see."

"Exactly," Merriman agreed. "So we'll stay here and see how things unfold."

"Do you think they might change their mind?" the lieutenant asked with a trace of hope in his voice.

Commander Merriman shook his head."They never do," he reminded him. And with this he went over to his horse, put his boot into the stirrup, and with the same ease he had shown when he dismounted, remounted and went back to the rearguard, raising another cloud of dust as he went.

Alex Riley went over to Sergeant Joaquín Alcántara. Taking his arm, he pointed at a spot twenty or thirty yards ahead.

"Jack, the Commander's given the order to set up camp here, so you take your squad and have them dig out a couple sniper trenches right there, by the olive trees."

"About time!" complained the Galician, wiping the sweat of his forehead with his sleeve. "It looked like they wanted to keep us marching right up to the village square."

"I wouldn't put it past them yet," Riley said with a humorless smile. "But for now we're going to settle our butts in the shade and rest till we get fresh orders."

"What did Merriman say?"

"Nothing. He's pissed at being here instead of marching on to Zaragoza, but he has to obey orders too."

"And what do you think?"

He looked toward Belchite, a mile and half ahead. It was a pretty village of closely-built stone houses with roofs of ochre tiles which in the distance and from their viewpoint on the north side appeared as compact and impenetrable as a wall.

"Is it going to be as tough as it looks?" he added.

Alex, looking in the same direction, put his hand on his friend's shoulder.

"Who knows? I've heard that we can count on air support as well as artillery, but even so… This village is like a medieval castle."

"The rumor says there are something like a thousand nationals entrenched in there. Many of them are Moors."

"That's what they say."

Jack looked at him out of the corner of his eye.

"That's a lot of nationals together, and the Moors'll fight to the end because they know if we capture them we'll shoot them."

"Well then, we'll have to kill them all," he replied coldly.

This time Jack turned to his superior. "Six months ago you wouldn't have said that," he murmured with veiled reproach.

The muscles in Alex's jaw tensed. "Six months ago," he said after a moment, without taking his gaze off the horizon, "I was a different person."

"Well, I liked the other one better, to be honest."

Riley turned to his second-in-command with rage flaring in his pupils. If it had been anyone else he would have had him arrested there and then. Even so, it took him a couple of seconds to get back his poise.

"You can go and look him up whenever you want," he said, barely holding back his annoyance. "He's buried at the foot of the Pingarrón along with the rest of his company. Murdered by the same ones who're hiding in that Godforsaken village."

"I know that, *carallo*. I was there too, remember? I'm the guy that dragged you out when you were bleeding to death with a shot in your chest."

Instinctively Alex raised his hand to the bullet scar beside his heart which had kept him in hospital in Valencia for four months, on the verge of death. But it was not that wound that stopped him sleeping at night and soiled his soul with a crust of resentment.

"That's enough chatter," he said sharply. "Do what I told you and don't take long about it. Before evening I want the whole section under cover."

"Yes sir, comrade lieutenant!" Joaquín Alcántara stood up straight, raising his fist to his forehead in a salute. He did it in such a ridiculously soldierly way it was impossible not to realize he was making fun of him.

"Go to hell, Jack," Riley muttered, before he turned to give orders to the remaining non-commissioned officers.

2

A couple of hours later the entire Lincoln Battalion had taken over the north side of a small hill dotted with olive trees, sheltered from the sun and the sightlines of the defenders of Belchite. These were certainly watching them through binoculars at that very moment, just as General Waclaw "Walter" Swierczewski was doing. He was a military man of Polish origin from the Red Army who had previously been in the Moscow Military Academy. Cold-eyed and inflexible in his attitude, he had been given absolute command of the International Brigades, which included the Lincoln Battalion.

Beside him, like a silent shadow, the political commissioner who had also been sent to the International Brigades, André Marty a sinister Frenchman with flickering eyes who was nicknamed "the Butcher of Albacete" stayed on the edge of things, watching and listening to everything with his hands behind his back.

"Comrade general," Merriman's powerful voice broke in suddenly.

"Yes?" replied General Walter without either turning round or taking his eyes from his binoculars.

"All the officers have arrived now. We can begin whenever you want."

"What's that?" he asked instead in his incomprehensible accent, pointing ahead.

Robert Merriman stood beside him shielding his eyes with his hand, trying to guess what he meant. "That big three-storied stone building with a bell tower? It's the Convent of San Rafael."

"Monks?"

"Nuns, I believe."

"I see. And that other one… right at the entrance to the village?"

"That's the Convent of San Agustín."

Now the general took his eyes from the binoculars and turned to the commander with a look of incredulity. "You must be joking. Two convents as big as that in such a small village?"

Merriman shrugged. *We're in Spain*, the gesture said. "We believe this one is abandoned."

General Walter put the binoculars back to his face and studied the building with renewed interest. "Interesting…" he murmured.

He took his time checking there were no artillery or bunkers near the village, and with a look of satisfaction he turned and went over to the small conclave waiting for him in a semicircle facing the side of a supply truck, on which they had hung a detailed map of the village and its surroundings.

"Comrades," he greeted the four captains and fifteen lieutenants who represented the entire officer staff of the Lincoln Battalion.

"Comrade general," they replied in unison as they stood to attention.

"At ease," Walter replied with a wave. Then, with hands crossed at his back, he stood in front of the map for two long minutes, turning his back on the officers, who waited silently for the general to speak."*Khorosho...Otlichno*" he said to himself in Russian, and nobody knew what it meant until he turned and repeated, "Good...Excellent."

The general in command of the International Brigades smiled, but there was nothing pleasant in that smile."American comrades," he said sweeping his gaze across them. "The Lincoln Battalion has been charged with the glorious mission of taking the village of Belvitche."

Beside him Merriman cleared his throat discreetly.

The general looked at him, then at the map, and corrected himself uninterestedly, "The village of Belchite. Whatever its name is, your mission will be to assault it from the north." He moved aside and rested his forefinger on the map. "These are our positions, and by tomorrow the noose around the village will be closed off by the troops under the command of Comrades Lister and Modesto, isolating them from the national supply lines. Then the air and artillery bombardments will begin, to soften the defenses, and in two or three days we'll begin the assault in which you'll take the initiative, going by this route" – he traced the thin black line which went past their own position and reached the north-eastern flank of the village – "taking these two buildings here first: an oil factory and an abandoned convent, which will be our bridgehead. Once you've made sure of your positions, another four divisions of tanks and infantry will attack on all flanks until we finish off any resistance." The trace of a smile appeared on his face, and clenching his fist he added, "and completely destroy the enemy."

The twenty-odd officers shifted uneasily, so Merriman hastened to add, "We're counting on four divisions, some twenty-four thousand men, as well as several units of artillery which will bomb the village continuously until the enemy forces are minimized. The High Command estimates that by the time we begin the assault, there will be almost no resistance."

"Comrade commander," said Michael Law. He was the first black officer in the history of the United States to lead a unit of white men and captain of the First Company, which included Riley. "What does *we'll take the initiative* mean exactly, and *once we've made sure of our positions, the remaining divisions will attack?*"

Merriman glanced at Walter before answering for him. "It means just what it means, captain. It's been decided that we'll begin the assault from the north, to distract the defenses so that the rest of the army can attack from the east and south."

Captain Law frowned. "I see…" he muttered. "Distract the defenses."

"Any problem with that, captain?" said the Polish general.

"No problem, comrade general," was the reply, with far-from-subtle sarcasm. "The Lincoln Battalion, as ever, is ready to go into battle on the front line."

General Walter's lips stretched in a cruel grin. "I'm very pleased to hear that, comrade captain," he replied with a piercing look. "Because you'll be happy to know that your own company will lead the initial assault."

"Understood, comrade general," Law said, raising his chin as if he were delighted with this order. Still, he was sufficiently prudent not to add anything else. He looked to his left and his eyes met Riley's, to whom he gestured an apology.

General Walter put his hands behind his back once more and remained silent for a few seconds, before he snapped out, "Any more questions?"

This time nobody dared express their doubts aloud, and Commander Merriman stepped in again, "We believe the defenders have about a thousand soldiers: volunteers, *requetés, falangistas,* and Moors. They might have some artillery hidden, which is why we can't begin the attack with the tanks. But as the general has just said, by the time we launch the assault the enemy forces will be weakened and they might already have surrendered."

In an involuntary reflex, Riley snorted. This did not pass unnoticed by the Polish general.

"Did you wish to say something, lieutenant?"

Someone beside him deliberately stepped on his foot. Even the commander himself seemed to be begging him to keep his mouth shut.

But keeping quiet had never been one of his virtues."Not really, comrade general. I was just thinking…" – he cleared his throat – "that we all know perfectly well the enemy isn't going to surrender. They know we nearly always shoot them, particularly the Moors, just as they do with us. So I wouldn't surrender if I was in their shoes and I wouldn't count on them doing it either. Wouldn't it be more sensible," he added, going beyond the limits of prudence, "to leave a corridor for the Nationals to leave by? We'd save plenty of lives, and it would be far easier to take the village. As my Spanish mother used to say: *If the enemy wants to flee, make it easy for them.*"

The general took two steps forward and the other officers moved back like the waters of the Red Sea. "Many thanks for sharing your mother's opinion on military tactics with us, lieutenant…"

"Riley, Alex Riley."

"Let me ask you something, Lieutenant Riley. Before enlisting in the International Brigades, what were you? What was your job?"

"I was an officer in the United States Merchant Navy, comrade general."

"A sailor… I see. And do you know what my profession was before I came to this war?"

"I have no idea, comrade general."

"I was a professor of high strategy at the Moscow Military Academy. What does that tell you?"

Alex seemed to think for a moment. "I don't know… That your students must be having a good vacation?"

Karol Waclaw Swiercewski blinked incredulously at the American's disrespectful reply. And then he smiled. Even the stupidest soldier of the regiment knew that this never meant anything good. "Commander," he said, turning abruptly toward Merriman, "we need a first-hand report on the enemy positions, so I want one of your men to get close to the village and give a detailed identification of the disposition of the defensive forces inside."

"Yes, comrade general."

"I recommend that this man," he added, turning briefly to Riley, "should be this ingenious lieutenant here. Tomorrow morning I want him to hand me a complete report at the command center, or else it will be you going out with the first patrol. Is that clear?"

"Crystal clear, comrade general."

"Excellent." Without another word he turned his back to the group of officers. He strode to the vehicle that was waiting for him a few yards away with his driver leaning on the hood, got in, and escorted by two motorcyclists, left at once, leaving behind a cloud of yellow dust.

The rest of the gathering dispersed in silence, going back to their units. Riley, however, felt a hand on his shoulder stopping him.

"You're a blabbermouth," came Law's voice beside him.

"Tell me something I don't know, captain."

"Why did you have to do it?"

For reply, Alex simply shrugged.

At that moment, Merriman, who had accompanied the general to his car, came back shaking his head. "What the hell were you thinking?" he burst out, spreading his hands wide. "Do you want the general to have you shot for insubordination?"

"He asked me and I gave him my opinion."

"Your opinion! Who cares about your opinion!" he cried angrily, jabbing his finger at Riley's chest. "You're here to obey orders and say yes to everything, not to give your opinions!"

"I thought—"

"Don't fucking think!"

Riley had a retort ready at the tip of his tongue, but he realized that Robert Merriman was upset because he genuinely appreciated him. "I beg your pardon, comrade commander," he said instead. "It won't happen again."

"Of course it won't happen again, you idiot." The tone of his voice did not change even after the apology. "You'll most probably be shot in that stupid patrol."

"I'll do everything in my power to avoid it."

"This time you really put your foot in it, Alex," Law said.

Merriman stared at him with much the same look he had given Riley. "You'd better shut up, Law. You've done enough too."

"Yes, comrade commander."

Merriman passed his hand over his forehead in a gesture of infinite weariness. "I can't believe the two best officers I have happen to be the stupidest in the entire Republican Army."

"Thank—"

"I told you to shut up, Law."

"Yes, sir."

Merriman began to walk in circles, shaking his head and snorting furiously at the same time. "Although you're such idiots, I'd like to do something to help. I might be able to convince the general that you've both apologized and have someone else go on the patrol. Maybe if you went to the command center in person—"

"Commander," Riley interrupted. "Bob."

Merriman stopped and looked up.

"Thank you, comrade commander," Alex added, "but don't do any of that. I'm not going to apologize to the general, and I don't want anybody else to take my place either. I'll lead that patrol and come back with the report. I got myself into this mess and I'll get out of it."

Merriman stared at the lieutenant of the First Company, then turned to look at the field separating them from the village of Belchite. It was a flat dry wasteland, dotted with olive trees and scrub, with scarcely anywhere to take cover and watch."I hope so," he said after a while and gave Riley's shoulder a friendly pat, but both his tone and his expression clearly showed that he doubted it.

3

The sun, swollen by dust and smoke, barely rose above the horizon under which it would disappear in a few minutes.

The hundred and ten men of the First Company were spread out over an area of fifty yards, grouped by sections around small fires and getting ready to sleep, most of them on their ragged, flea-ridden blankets.

Beside one of those fires, his gaze fixed on the dry crackling of the olive wood burning there, Alex Riley was sitting on the ground with his legs crossed, meticulously checking the mechanism of his Colt pistol when Joaquín Alcántara said beside him, "You're a bloody fool."

"That's the third time you've said it, Jack."

"You're a bloody fool."

Riley clicked the safety catch and put the gun in its holster. "That's enough, sergeant."

The Galician snorted. It was clear he did not agree. "Is that why I risked my life at the Pingarrón? Just so that you could go and commit suicide?"

Riley looked at him out of the corner of his eye. "Don't be melodramatic, Jack. You're acting like my mother."

"If I was your mother I'd have given you what for already."

Alex raised his eyes and saw that Shelby, Honeycombe and Fisher, the other sergeants of the section who were sitting beside them, as well as half a dozen corporals, were watching them attentively, not missing a word of the conversation. "Sergeant Alcántara," he said, suddenly serious, "one more word and I'll have you arrested."

"Bloody fool," the other repeated defiantly.

Riley decided that even though this was his best friend, he could not allow such a lack of respect in front of the other non-commissioned officers, so he jumped up to tell him he was under arrest.

But at that moment the figure of Commander Merriman burst into the circle of firelight, and it was noticeable that he was even more impeccably dressed than usual. He smiled broadly and with a firm step approached Riley as if they had not seen each other in years. "Good evening, comrade Lieutenant Riley," he said, and clasped his hand.

Alex returned the handshake in puzzlement, trying to hide his surprise. "Good evening… comrade Commander Merriman."

"Everything ready for your mission?"

"My mission? Yes… sure, I guess."

"Good to hear it! Good to hear it!" he replied with exaggerated vehemence. He looked like a bad actor in his first audition, overacting.

"Are you all right, commander?" The question he had in mind was whether he was drunk, but for once his prudence was faster than his tongue.

"Perfectly!" he replied. "I was going around to cheer the troops and I thought I'd come and wish you luck before you set off."

This was getting even weirder. "Oh, well… thank you, comrade."

"Call me Bob. Brave men can call me Bob, lieutenant."

"Of course, command—"

"Let me introduce you to a couple of friends who've come to visit us, Alex," he interrupted, and moving aside he signaled two civilians who were waiting a few yards away to come closer.

It was nothing out of the ordinary for politicians of the Republican government to come to the front during the days prior to an attack, surrounded by photographers and as slickers, wrongly believing that by doing this they were encouraging the soldiers to fight more determinedly. But those two civilians were not politicians at all. They were a man and a woman, both as tall as Riley, and from afar he could identify a certain determination in their way of walking that was typical of his own fellow country people.

The man was big, red-faced, with an intense gaze behind a pair of round glasses, a modest moustache in accord with the black beret covering his head and a knotted tie worn with an old gray shirt soiled with dust and blood.

The woman was a blonde with apparently endless legs shrouded in loose trousers, which nevertheless stirred admiration and not a few whistles from the men as she passed by. Her intelligent blue eyes stood out in a face that was definitely more striking than beautiful. One glance was enough to let you sense that she had a strong and independent personality.

"Lieutenant Riley," Merriman said with the trace of a nod, "let me introduce you to Mr. Ernest Hemingway, from the *North American Newspaper Alliance,* and Miss Martha Gellhorn, from the magazine *Collier's Weekly.* They're both well-known American journalists, sympathetic to our cause."

Alex shook their hands, still blinking in confusion."Pleased to meet you."

"The pleasure is all ours," Hemingway said in a deep baritone. "It's always an honor to meet a brave man."

Alex Riley did not know what to say to this. He nodded with a glance at Merriman, trying to gauge what he might have told them and what the hell was going on.

Gellhorn seemed to guess his puzzlement. Coming to Alex's side, with a sensuality which – whether real or imaginary – was somehow unsettling, she said, "Ernest and I have come to cover the attack on Belchite, Lieutenant Riley, and over dinner with your commander he told us about you and your heroism in the Battle of Jarama, and the fact that tonight you're planning to infiltrate the enemy lines all by yourself to gather information."

Riley looked at Merriman again, and this time his commander winked at him conspiratorially."Is that what he said?" Alex said with a grimace. "Well, I'm sorry to say that things aren't always what they seem. I'm not a hero, nor do I want to be."

Martha Gellhorn smiled faintly."That's what the commander told us you'd say."

"The reply of a true hero," said Hemingway.

Riley shook his head tiredly."Do you know the real definition of a hero?" he asked both of them. "Someone who manages to get everybody around him dead."

"Okay, okay," Hemingway said, giving in. He went over to Riley and put his arm around his shoulders with crushing familiarity. "Let's not argue about that, shall we?" And with a gesture at the ground he added, "Why don't we get comfortable and chat for a while?"

Riley could smell the whisky on the journalist's breath."I'm not in the mood," he replied.

Gellhorn put a hand on his arm."Please… lieutenant."

Riley turned toward his commander, but Merriman's look made it clear that he had to put up with it.

"Lieutenant," he said by way of an extra threat, "look after our guests while I deal with a few dispatches. Their articles are worth as much as tanks in this war. I'll be back shortly." With a slight nod, he walked away.

Alex looked around for Jack in search of moral support, but his friend only had eyes for the blond journalist.

They had already sat down."We'd like to talk to you," she said, taking out a small pocket notebook. "Tell us about your experience as a volunteer in this war."

"My experience?" he asked also sitting down, reluctantly.

"How you feel," Hemingway said. "Why you fight. Who you fight for."

Riley stared at the burly journalist before he answered."I fight for them." He pointed at the men around the fire. "So they can go back home safe and sound."

"And for the cause, of course," added Hemingway.

Alex looked askance at him, but kept silent.

"And what about the war?" Gellhorn asked. "Do you think you're going to win?"

Riley picked a pebble from the ground and threw it into the fire, apparently distracted, as if he had not heard the question. There was a cloud of sparks. "Nobody's going to win this war," he said finally, in a weary voice. "Whatever happens, everyone's going to lose."

"That's not what I was expecting to hear," Martha admitted.

"Do you want a speech about freedom, democracy and things like that?"

"About decency, perhaps. Justice. Morals…"

"Those words have no place in war, Miss Gellhorn."

"Then don't you have any ideals?" Hemingway put in. "Aren't you fighting against fascism?"

"Don't give me that crap. Those are the words used by the soulless people who organize the wars, to convince idiots like us to enlist."

"But you're a volunteer. You enlisted to fight for the cause."

"The reasons why I enlisted are my business."

"Not all wars are the same, lieutenant."

Riley took a deep breath before replying. "No, not all of them, and that's why I volunteered to fight in this one. But in the end, in this one and in all of them, you find out there's only blood, pain and shit. If you're looking for high-falutin' concepts and ideologies, you've come to the wrong place."

"In case you didn't know, I was a soldier too," said Hemingway, rather upset. "So don't try to teach me any lessons."

"I know you were in the Great War, Mr. Hemingway... driving an ambulance," Riley replied.

The journalist's expression changed quickly. "You know who I am?"

"Of course I do. I read *A Farewell to Arms*. Or rather I tried, because I couldn't finish it. I was bored stiff."

The writer stared at him arrogantly. "Not everybody can appreciate a good book."

"Maybe, but it's still a bore."

Hemingway rose, reeling a little. "Do you want to fight, buddy?" he asked as he rolled up his sleeves. "I've broken noses for less than that."

"Sit down, Ernest!" Gellhorn said in a tone of authority. "We've come to talk to the lieutenant, not for you to get into a fight with him."

"Don't worry," Alex said nonchalantly. "I never fight drunks unless I'm drunk too."

Hemingway lunged at Riley. "I'm going to—"

Before he could take the first step, Joaquín Alcántara leapt up like a spring and materialized before him out of nowhere.

"What the hell?" muttered the journalist.

"Easy, pal," Jack said putting a hand on the other's chest. "Why don't you come for a stroll with me? I really liked your novel."

"Hey you, leave me alone. I'm not going—"

"Come this way," Jack insisted. Grabbing his arm and ignoring his protests, he almost dragged him away. "I'll introduce you to the rest of the company."

"But—"

The last thing they heard as they walked away was Jack asking. "You lived in Paris, didn't you? Is it true what they say about French women?"

Riley and Gellhorn remained seated, watching the Galician lead the journalist away.

"I apologize for Ernest's behavior, lieutenant."

Riley brushed it off."It doesn't matter. I was really the one who provoked him."

Gellhorn frowned."And why did you do that? Do you realize his articles are the most widely read in the United States?"

"Yeah, I know. But for him it's just another war. He's always talking about courage, heroes and ideals, but when most of us here are dead and rotting in some trench, he'll be on his boat fishing for marlin off the coast of Florida, with a glass of whisky in one hand and a cigar in the other."

"That's his job," she said. "He's a journalist, like me. We tell what we see so that the world knows about it. We're the witnesses to what's happening here."

"So what? Nothing's going to change, no matter what they do or what they say. The fact is that nobody cares."

"My readers care. Otherwise they wouldn't read my articles."

Riley shook his head."Forgive me for saying this, but for the readers your articles are just a distraction, an entertainment between the society page and the sports page. The great majority doesn't give a damn about who's fighting and why in this civil war."

Gellhorn was about to respond angrily, but her reply died on the tip of her tongue."You might be right," she said instead, gazing at the weathered faces of the soldiers lying around the fire. "Perhaps I'm just part of the show. Like the theater critic who writes about a play and then goes home to sleep." She turned to Riley and studied him carefully for the first time: the hard profile of his weathered, sunburned face, his straight nose, his black hair, his almond eyes reflecting the light of the fire. "What will you do when the war ends?" she asked.

Riley shrugged. "I don't think about that."

"So, what do you think about, lieutenant?"

"About the ocean."

"The ocean?" she repeated in surprise.

"Ever since I came to Spain I haven't seen the ocean again, you know? I dream of it every day, of sailing a long way from dry land. Going very far away. Choosing a point on the horizon and heading toward it without telling anybody or worrying about leaving anything behind." He turned to her and stared into those beautiful blue eyes which were studying him so intently. "Although right now I was thinking that… in another place and other circumstances, I'd invite you out for dinner in some quiet place, then I'd take you dancing… and finally I'd suggest that we go to a hotel and spend the night together."

Gellhorn's cheeks reddened, but she kept her gaze firm as she answered him in a low voice, "And I'd be delighted to accept." She looked around and drew her face close to Riley's so that the other men would not hear her. "You try to come back in one piece tonight, lieutenant, and we'll see what can be done."

4

When Sergeant Alcántara came back to the fire at Riley's section, he found him already finishing his preparations. He had put on a dark shirt Honeycombe had lent him and painted his face and hands with shoe polish, and was now doing the same to his belt buckle and studs.

"How's Hemingway?" he asked Jack when he saw him arrive.

"Pissed off. He was saying something about challenging you to a duel, but by tomorrow he won't remember a thing." Jack smiled. "I left him in the commander's tent. He can deal with his own guests." As he spoke, he picked up the can of shoe polish and began to paint his own face.

"And how did you get along with the blonde? You can't complain about the favor I did you when I left you two alone."

Instead of answering, Alex stared at his second-in-command with a frown. "What do you think you're doing?"

"What does it look like? Protecting my delicate skin."

"Leave that shoe polish where it was, Jack. This time I'm going alone."

"Sure, sure…" his friend replied without stopping what he was doing.

"I mean it. You're not coming. That's an order."

Jack's smile stood out against his blackened face."Do you really want me to spell out where you can put that order?"

"Don't fuck with me, Jack. It's stupid for you to come. The two of us would be more easily spotted. You're staying, and that's it."

The sergeant came to stand in front of the lieutenant, arms akimbo, staring at him defiantly."Whatever you say, I'm coming with you, so stop wasting time trying to order me around. It's nearly eleven by now, and we should've left half an hour ago."

"I could have you arrested."

"And I could kick you in the balls."

For a moment Riley considered arresting his friend. It was true that two of them would be more easily spotted. But it was also true that if there were any trouble, there was nobody else he would rather have beside him."All right then. Leave everything but your gun and knife. No ammunition or water. Empty your bladder and make sure anything metallic is covered in shoe polish." He patted his shoulder. "We leave in five minutes."

"I only need three," Jack said.

In fact ten minutes went by before Captain Michael Law came up to them to give them last-minute instructions. Standing before them, he studied them from top to toe. They were completely clad and disguised in black except for the whites of their eyes, which stood out exaggeratedly on their faces. "Would it be too much to ask you not to play around more than usual tonight?" he asked. "Go out there and take a look without running any unnecessary risks. Most likely there'll be patrols around the village, and if you stumble on one of those you'll be in serious trouble, so keep your eyes wide open. Understood?"

"Right, comrade captain," Riley said with a nod.

"I just want you to get close enough to get an idea of the forces occupying the abandoned monastery and the oil factory, and try to find out whether they've got any artillery or heavy machineguns hidden. Nothing more. Is that clear?"

"Don't worry, captain," Jack said with a smile, so that a row of white teeth appeared on his broad face. "I promise we won't try to take Belchite all on our own."

The Afro-American officer glanced at his watch, then turned his head toward the east, where the waning moon had just appeared. "It's a bad night for a foray," he said with a grimace. "Too much moon and not a cloud in the sky… but that's the situation. Remember, dawn's at half past seven, so if you're not back before seven, you'll be like sitting ducks in the middle of the field. Is that clear?"

"Absolutely clear," Riley replied. "We'll be back way before that, I hope," he added. He stared at Jack, whose face still showed the white line of his teeth. "What are you so happy about?"

"I beg your pardon, comrade captain," he answered. He was making a visible effort to remain serious. "But I can't help thinking that with Alex and me painted the way we are… now you're the least black of the three of us."

They were able to cover the first five hundred yards at a crouch, taking advantage of the olive trees, rocks and trenches to hide from sight of the defenders. But from there on, between them and the north boundary of the village, there was nothing but barren, abandoned fields without a single bush to hide behind.

They studied the awkward situation before them."What does it look like?" Riley asked Jack, both looking at the horizon through small field binoculars.

The sergeant glanced sideways at Riley before replying."Very black," he said, his mouth twitching into a smile.

Alex turned aside from the front to look at his friend."Come on, stop joking. I'm serious."

Jack suppressed the smile and raised his head a few inches above the undergrowth."This fucks everything up," he whispered. "There's almost nowhere to hide from here to the first houses. If we go straight across the field, they'll see us for sure."

"I was thinking the same." He put the binoculars back to his face and turned his attention to his left. "But there's a farm over there. About four hundred yards away."

Jack looked in the same direction."Looks like a good place. Although who's to say there won't be a whole platoon of legionnaires lurking inside, waiting for some fool to walk past them?"

"All the more reason to get over there to nose around. If that's the case, we can't let them stay so close to our lines."

"Sure… but how are we going to get there? Crawling on our bellies for a quarter of a mile? There's nothing but flat land all the way."

"That's the best part. Look." He pointed to a long scar that cleft the ground and disappeared into the night in the direction of the house.

"An irrigation ditch."

"If we crawl on all fours, we'll be able to get close without being seen."

The robust Galician thought about this plan for several seconds, not relishing the thought of crawling for such a distance. "All right," he said at last, seeing that it was the best option. Half-bowing, he added, "Ladies first."

The water which in spring must have run along the ditch had evaporated long ago, and now it was just a rut less than twenty inches deep, scattered with rubble and brushwood.

They crawled on in the dark, almost blind, as the reflection of the moon did not reach the bottom, so that every now and then one or other of them would muffle a moan as he stabbed his hands on a thorn.

"*Cagüenla…*" Jack swore for the umpteenth time when they were nearly ten minutes into their journey.

"Shhh…" hissed Alex, turning to him and putting his finger to his lips. "We're very close. Shut up."

To check, Jack peered out and saw that this was correct. Not far away they saw a cottage with rough stone walls and thatched roof, small windows and a wooden shed at the back. Around it, there were scattered hoes, forks and other farm tools.

"Seems like nobody's home," murmured Jack, checking that not a sound or crack of light was coming out from inside.

By way of answer, Riley pointed at the chimney. From it a thin thread of white smoke, barely perceptible, was issuing. "Let's go around the house," he whispered, miming with his hand.

Jack nodded in agreement and followed Riley out of the ditch, dragging himself along with the greatest care.

They did not stand up until they reached the shed, close to its wall. They waited a moment to check everything was still calm. Then, crouching as low as they could, they reached the back of the house.

There was only a single window, too high to let them look inside, so, hugging the wall like two huge black lizards, they rounded the corner.

However, on that side of the house there was a pair of large windows, one of them wide open, like an invitation to peer inside.

Riley and Jack exchanged looks. Almost on tiptoe they approached the open window until they were right under it. They took out their weapons and cocked them carefully to muffle the sound of the hammer. Then, leaning against the wall, very slowly, they peered over the windowsill like a pair of common snoops.

The inside of the house was completely dark. Scarcely any light reached inside, but the fact that there were no soldiers watching inside or out reassured Riley sufficiently to let him straighten up carefully and put his head through the window.

Gradually his sight accustomed itself to the deep darkness, and he was able to make out shapes and large objects. This was the living room, with a big table occupying the center of the room with half a dozen rustic chairs around it and old photos of ancestors hanging on whitewashed walls, while above a fireplace where the last embers still glowed, a huge pot was hanging with its lid half off, emitting a pungent aroma of stew.

Riley felt his stomach growl and, unable to stop himself, he began to drool like a lion at the sight of a fawn. It had been weeks since he had eaten anything decent apart from the disgusting mess rations, and the smell of that stew was giving him goosebumps.

Then he became aware that Jack had stood up and was getting ready to clamber in through the window. "What the hell are you doing?" he spat out, grabbing the other's sleeve.

Jack looked at Riley as if he had forgotten he was there. "Umm... I'm going to... investigate... you know..." he muttered, his eyes fixed on the pot.

"Are you out of your mind? We can't go in like thieves and steal their food."

"No, I just want to... I want to taste it..." he said, putting one leg across.

"For Christ's sake, Jack!" Riley said raising his voice without realizing. "Stop! They're going to—" His voice broke off as he heard the dull sound of a door slamming behind him.

5

The blood froze in Riley's veins. He was paralyzed, realizing they had been discovered and that there was probably a gun pointed at their backs. Out of the corner of his eye he saw that Jack had completely lost his appetite, and guessed he had turned white under the layer of black shoe polish on his face.

They were both petrified, Jack with half his body inside the house and Alex clutching his sleeve. Any sudden move might get them shot right there and then, in a very unheroic situation.

"Hello!" came an unexpectedly nonchalant voice. "Who are you?"

Alex and Jack exchanged incredulous looks. They turned around very slowly and met the questioner.

A boy of about eight, barefoot and wearing a stained, heavily patched nightshirt, was looking at them curiously at the door of the filthy latrine he had just emerged from. "Are you thieves?" he asked. He had a huge mop of matted black hair, inquisitive dark eyes and a collection of stains on his face which were visible even in the inadequate moonlight. "Are you black men from Africa?" he added.

Jack lowered his leg from the window, while Alex stepped forward and crouched down to appear less intimidating, although in fact the boy did not seem in the least intimidated. "No, we're not black men from Africa," he said, lowering his voice in the hope that the boy would do the same. "We're friends."

"Whose friends?"

"Your friends, for example."

"How can you be my friends if you just met me?"

Jack stifled a laugh.

"Well, you see," Alex went on, ignoring the sergeant, "my name is Alex, and this fat man here is my friend Joaquín. And you? What's your name?"

"Javier Antonio López Reverte."

"Hello, Javier Antonio," he said, and held out his hand.

The boy shook it with a firmness unusual for his age.

"Now we can be friends."

The boy, however, was frightened when he looked at his hand and saw that it was now black. "You've made me black!" He raised his voice in alarm. "I don't want to be black!"

Alex made a peremptory gesture to make him keep his voice down, and rubbed his hand on his shirt to show him there was white skin underneath. The boy had probably never seen any other skin color but his own, nor had anybody explained to him that skin color is not contagious.

"Don't worry Javier, it's just shoe polish. See? Don't shout, please."

"Are your parents at home, Javier?" Jack asked.

"Sleeping," the boy replied when he had regained his calm.

"And… is there anybody else?"

"My sisters Juana and Josefa. But they're very small and can't talk properly."

"I mean… someone else who isn't part of the family? Soldiers, for example?"

The boy shook his head. "They came two days ago, but they left straight away."

"I see…" Alex said with a nod. "Could you tell your father that we're here, and that we'd like to talk to him? Tell him we're frien…" He thought about this and added, "Better not to say anything. Just take us to him."

With the boy walking ahead of them they went into the house, sat down at the table and lit an oil lamp. The boy went to wake his parents.

At once they heard muffled voices from the next room. Voices of a man and a woman, varying from disbelief to concern.

A minute later the gaunt, unkempt face of a sleepy man peered at them, with the expression of someone not quite sure whether he was still in the middle of a bad dream. "Good evening," he whispered in a rough, hoarse voice, trying in vain to make himself decent by stuffing the tail of his nightshirt into his pants. "Who are you?"

"Good evening, my good man," Alex said, wiping the shoe polish from his face with his shirtsleeve. "We're two soldiers of the Republican Army, and we don't want to cause you any trouble. We were on patrol and saw your house.

We'd just come to take a closer look when your son chanced on us."

As Riley was saying this, the man sat down in front of them with his gaze still blurred by sleep. "And what do you want... from me?" he asked. "You can see we're poor, and we've got next to nothing. Some Moorish soldiers took our hens... I got nothing to give you."

Jack cleared his throat at once and looked at the pot, from which emanated a delicious smell of stew.

Alex, though, shook his head.

"No, Mr..."

"Eustaquio López Ledesma, at your service."

"Mr. López. We haven't come to take anything, don't you worry. I just want to ask you a few questions."

"I don't know nothing."

"Easy, my friend," Jack said, noticing their host's nervousness and trying out his best smile. "This isn't an interrogation, and there's no need for you to worry. Relax, nothing's going to happen to you or your family."

Eustaquio seemed to believe his words. "Maybe *you* don't," he said nodding toward the closed window which gave on to the village, "but if they find out you've come to my house..."

"Don't you worry about that either," Riley said to reassure him. "Nobody saw us arrive and nobody will see us leave."

"We'd like to know," Jack said, coming to the point, "whether you've been into the village lately."

The man shook his head. "I haven't been to the village in a long time. I'm afraid to leave my wife alone with the kids, you know, what with so many soldiers around. I heard the Moors…" He left it at that.

"So you wouldn't know how many soldiers there are, or if they have any artillery or mortars?"

"Cannons? Yes, they have some. I saw them when I went to sell a few eggs. But I don't know nothing about weapons."

"And soldiers? Were there a lot of them?"

Eustaquio nodded."Thousands. More than there are people in the village. They've occupied nearly all the buildings in the center, the hospital and the Convent of San Agustín."

The two soldiers exchanged worried looks. If what the villager was saying was true, the defenders were more numerous and better-equipped than the High Command supposed. This information was not what the general was expecting, but there was no doubt it would be all the more valuable.

"Many thanks, my friend," Riley said, nodding in acknowledgement. "What you've told us might save many lives. But… what I don't understand," he added with a frown, "is why you're still here. There's been fighting in Quinto and Codo, just a few miles from here. You should've left days ago."

The villager shrugged."Go? Where to? This house is all we have," he said, waving his hand around. "If we leave, we'll lose it. I can't make it to the mountains with the wife and three kids."

At that moment, the wife appeared, wearing a long nightgown and with her hair in a hastily arranged bun which revealed a face that was still young, though marked with premature wrinkles and bags under her eyes. She was carrying a jug of wine and three glasses, which she left on the table. Then, without a word, she went back to the bedroom.

Jack and Riley nodded gratefully at the woman, and Alex said gravely, "A young wife, three children and your own life. That's exactly what you're going to lose if you don't get away."

"There's nowhere to go, I've told you," the man insisted.

Jack leaned on the table, pushing the jug aside."Look, Eustaquio. I don't think you really understand the situation." He breathed in before adding, "The Republican Army has completely surrounded Belchite, ready to destroy it, and if there are as many Nationals as you say, they'll defend themselves with tooth and claw and there'll be a terrible battle… and you're right in the middle of it all."

The look on the peasant's face was guarded, but there was still a trace of doubt in his eyes.

"In a few days," Riley said, waving his hand around him, "this house will be a pile of rubble. The only difference will be whether you and your family are underneath it or not."

"But we've done nothing… we're farmers…" he protested, almost beseechingly. "Can't be. S'not fair."

"War's unfair, my friend. But you still have a chance of escaping with your family. Take it. Tonight." He turned to Jack, and added, "We'll help you cross the enemy lines without being stopped."

The man was about to object again, but he said nothing, and looked down at the table with a tired gesture."I can't leave…" he said at last in a faint voice.

"Didn't you hear what I just told you? Belchite's going to be destroyed, and this farm with it."

"I heard you perfectly well," he replied, lifting his eyes and fixing them on Alex. "And that's just why I can't leave. My whole family and my wife's are still in the village. I can't leave without them."

Jack regretted in advance what he was about to say. "You have no choice, pal. Get used to the idea that they… well."

A flash of rage shone in the villager's eyes. "Don't you say that," he said furiously. "They're my parents, my brothers and my sisters, and my wife's. I'm not going to leave them and run away."

"If you stay, you'll die too."

Eustaquio's face hardened. "Not if I take them with me."

Alex and Jack wondered if they had heard right.

"I'll go get them," the man insisted, "and tomorrow night we'll all go together."

Riley rubbed his eyes in exhaustion. "Listen, my friend. I don't mean to ruin your party, but what you're saying is crazy. How many people are we talking about?"

Eustaquio took a moment to make a quick calculation with his fingers. After a long minute, he said, "Nine or ten."

"Nine or ten?" Jack repeated. "How the hell are you going to take ten people out of the village without being seen?"

"I dunno," he admitted, and shrugged. "But strike me dead if I don't have a go. If you was in my place, wouldn't you want to save your family?"

Riley crossed his arms and sat back in the rough wooden chair. "All right then," he growled. "Do whatever you want. But do it before the bombing starts, because otherwise you won't be able to get away."

"Tomorrow I'll send the lad to the village to warn the family. Nobody'll suspect him. I'll ask them to come here tomorrow night and we'll cross the Republican lines together."

"Okay," Riley said with a nod. He stood up and offered him his hand. "I wish you all the luck in the world."

The villager stared at him in puzzlement. "Aren't you going to help us? You said you'd help us cross your lines."

"What?" Alex asked in surprise.

"You said you'd help us," Eustaquio insisted, opening his eyes wide.

"But—"

"You just told me! You're a couple of liars!"

"*Carallo...*" muttered Joaquín Alcántara.

Riley raised his hands in a soothing gesture. "Okay then. Okay…" He glanced at Jack. "You gather all your people here, and tomorrow night at the same time we'll come and help you have free passage to the crossroads at Fuentes de Ebro. Okay?"

The man's face lit up as if the Virgin Mary had appeared before him. "Thanks very much," he said, taking first Alex's hands and then Jack's in his own. "God bless you!"

"Don't thank us yet," said Alex gravely. "You just make sure the Nationals don't find out anything, because if they discover you they'll most likely shoot you all. Do you understand?"

"Yes, yes… of course. They won't realize. Tomorrow we'll be here waiting."

"And don't you let anybody bring anything but the clothes they wear and some food and water in a bundle," Jack emphasized, getting to his feet in his turn. "No belongings or mementoes or junk. Only people. You're not moving house."

"Sure, sure…" Eustaquio repeated. He made to embrace both men, but held back at the last minute as he remembered all the shoe polish that covered them. "But please don't go yet. Aren't you hungry?"

The lieutenant shook his head. "We're in the middle of a mission… even though it might not look like it. We have to go now."

The farmer indicated the big smoking pot. "But my wife has made a stew to die for," he said, "and somewhere here I've got a *bota* filled with good wine. What d'you say?"

Riley was about to decline the offer for the second time, but when he opened his mouth Jack stepped on him so hard under the table that he almost crushed his foot.

6

Dawn the following day found Alex Riley covering the handful of miles which separated him from the command post. In an olive-green 8HP Ford he sat in the seat beside Commander Merriman while a quartermaster corporal drove, not too skillfully, along a narrow dusty dirt road.

"I love your car, Bob," Alex said, running his hand along the window frame. "The day this war ends and I go back home, I think I'll buy one like it."

Robert Merriman glanced at him, but his thoughts seemed to be very far away. "Yes," he answered vaguely. "It's a good automobile."

Riley was no fool, and he could guess why his commander was lost in thought. When they had come back from their patrol and he had passed on what the villager had told him about the enemy forces in Belchite, his expression had changed as if he had seen a ghost.

Unexpectedly, Merriman turned to the lieutenant and asked him in a whisper, "Do you think we'll win this war?"

Riley stared at his commander and friend. He would never have expected him to ask such a question, least of all in the moments prior to an attack. To gain time, he thought of asking him what he meant, and for once decided to be careful with his words. "I'm not really the right person to give an opinion on something so—"

"Stop the crap, Alex. I'm asking you as a friend. Do you believe we'll win?"

Riley took a deep breath and waited a few seconds before answering. "If we manage to resist until the inevitable war in Europe starts, we'll have a chance. If Hitler goes into war against France and Great Britain, the government of the Republic will join the allies, and we'll be able to count on their help fighting Franco and his Nazi friends."

Merriman nodded in agreement, but then asked again, "And if not? What if Hitler's waiting for this war to end before he starts his own?"

Now it was Alex's turn to stare at his commander in puzzlement. "Why are you asking me all this? You know I'm not a soldier. I'm just a sailor in the middle of a war that's not even his own."

Merriman smiled wearily. "Because I trust you, Alex. I trust your good judgment and your honesty, more than these morons in the High Command or all the fanatic generals. I don't get many chances to ask someone with a mind of his own."

Again Alex thought twice before answering, but then decided to speak his mind. "If we're lucky, we might not lose it," he said. "But as things stand now, there's not much we can do against an army much better equipped and organized than ours."

Merriman nodded again, in silence.

"And what do you think, Bob?" Riley wanted to know in turn. "Do we stand a chance?"

The commander gave Alex a long look, apparently meditating whether to answer him or not. When he was about to do so, the car stopped abruptly by a great tent surrounded by armed men and sacks of dirt, where the Republican flag fluttered alongside that of the International Brigades.

Inside the tent, sitting at the table and gulping down fried eggs and chorizo, General Walter was so absorbed in his breakfast he did not notice their arrival.

Behind him the political commissary André Marty stood like a diligent waiter, and in the furthest corner of the tent a soldier stood to attention staring ahead and stoically enduring the delicious smell of food which filled the air.

"Comrade General," Merriman said, coming to stand in front of him and saluting him with a nod.

Walter gestured to him to sit in the only free chair, without taking his attention from the plate in front of him.

Riley remained standing to attention beside Merriman.

"Have you had your breakfast yet, commander?" the general asked. "Would you like me to order anything for you? The eggs are delicious."

"No thank you, comrade general. I had breakfast in the camp," he lied.

The Pole did not even look at Riley, as if he were a dog waiting by the table.

"Good, good… and tell me, do you have the report I asked from you?"

"I do indeed, comrade general. Last night, Lieutenant Riley carried out an incursion that brought him into contact with a few civilians, who provided him with some very important information."

The general, who had not stopped eating while the other spoke, paused for a moment. Without letting go of his fork, he raised an eyebrow with interest.

"It seems," said Merriman, "that the rebel forces are far greater than was estimated at the start. The information the lieutenant gathered last night tells of several thousand men, as well as a fair amount of artillery. A lot more than the thousand men and two or three cannon the High Command spoke about."

Now General Karol Waclaw looked at Riley with suspicion. "You say a civilian gave you this information?"

"That's correct, comrade general. A farmer," he replied, his gaze still fixed ahead.

"A farmer…" Walter ruminated, leaving the fork on the unfinished plate. "And you… did you by any chance see these troops? Those thousand men and numerous cannon they spoke about?"

Riley took a deep breath before answering. It was easy to guess where the conversation was heading. "Not personally, comrade general. After I heard this I decided it was more important to come back to base and report to my commander."

The general picked up his napkin and wiped his mouth, leaving stains of chorizo grease on it.

"So, let's see…" he said, sitting back in his chair." You go out on patrol, but instead of crossing the enemy lines to get the information as you were ordered to, what you do is talk to an illiterate peasant who tells you a story about thousands of National soldiers of whom we have no record, and you expect... well, what exactly is it that you expect, lieutenant? That I believe you? Are you going to try to persuade me of the existence of Santa Claus while you're at it?"

The political commissary Marty giggled like a hyena, getting on Riley's nerves.

"Comrade general, you don't—" he began to say, clenching his fists.

Merriman interrupted him brusquely, perhaps fearing his reply would be impertinent. "I think we should consider the information the lieutenant has brought us," he argued, diverting attention to himself. "The source might be dubious, but it wouldn't hurt to take it into account. If it turns out to be true, the attack might be much more complicated than we were expecting."

"Are you hinting that we should delay the attack, commander?" Waclaw said, spelling out the words slowly to emphasize his question. "Perhaps cancel it altogether?"

"Not at all, comrade general."

"Because of what a poor peasant has *supposedly*"– Riley did not like the way he spoke the word – "told this officer? What if the peasant is a spy? Uh? Did you consider that?" The general's finger was pointing at Merriman like the barrel of a gun. "Who's to say he's not a fascist agent trying to delay our plans? Did you consider that?"

"No, sir," Merriman admitted. "I didn't consider that, comrade general."

"You see?" the other replied smugly, leaning forward across the table. "That's why comrade Stalin put me in charge." He put his finger to his temple and added, "Because I think."

"Of course, comrade general."

"And I think," he added without being prompted, "that this peasant is a fascist agent who's trying to undermine our morale. So not a word to anyone. Understood?"

"As you say, comrade general."

"You may go now." He shook his hand like someone swatting away a fly. "Because of you, my eggs have gone cold."

Merriman did not need to hear the order twice to leap to his feet, anxious to leave the tent as soon as possible. But halfway to the exit he realized Riley was still fixed on the spot, his fists clenched so tight his knuckles were white.

"Lieutenant!" he called, fearing the worst.

But Riley had eyes only for the overweight general renewing the attack on his breakfast. "Comrade general," he said under his breath, "I request permission to speak."

The general raised his eyes to look at the American officer. Strong and tall but not too muscular, his untidy black hair, longer than regulation allowed, framed a suntanned face whose most notable features were inquisitive amber eyes and a wide jaw, locked so tight it looked about to burst. "No," he replied with a disdainful look. "You do not have permission to speak. And get out before I have you arrested."

"The man I spoke with wasn't a fascist spy, comrade general," Riley said, despite this. He was now staring steadily into the Pole's eyes. "The lives of hundreds of soldiers might depend on this information, which I can't assure you is true but which doesn't have to be anything else. Because what I am sure of is that he wasn't an enemy agent."

To Riley's surprise it was Commissary Marty who spoke, interrupting the expletive forming in the general's lips."And 'ow do you know?" he squeaked shrilly with an exaggerated French accent. "Maybe you are an expert in military intelligence and interrogations, and you 'adn't told us?"

Riley ignored the mockery implied in the question and made an effort to stay calm."Tonight they're going to try to escape toward our lines. If they were fascists, they'd be heading for Zaragoza."

The commissary made a sign to indicate that he had not heard properly."Zey will try? Do you mean to say…zere were more zan one?"

"A family, comrade commissary. A frightened farmer and his wife, with three small children."

The commissary seemed to be assessing this information carefully."I see…" He stroked his chin and asked, "And you say zey want to escape by crossing our lines? 'Ow?"

Riley swallowed."I… promised to help them."

An unpleasant smile formed on André Marty's lips.

"Repeat that," General Walter ordered, his face turning crimson with rage. "You're going to help a possible enemy agent to cross our defenses? Did I hear right?"

"Comrade general," Merriman intervened, moving to stand beside Riley, "I beg you to ignore the lieutenant's words. He's still recovering from some serious wounds he took in the Battle of Jarama, and his medication makes him say things he doesn't really mean. Besides, he's under great stress, and he's spent the night carrying out the mission he was given. I can assure you he's a good soldier, loyal to the Republic" – he flashed a brief glance at Riley – "and he'd never do anything like what you just insinuated. I'm sure he only meant to make you understand how trustworthy his source is, but there's no way he'd do anything as stupid as helping a stranger cross our lines. Isn't that right, lieutenant?" he asked, this time turning to him.

Alex Riley took a second longer than necessary to reply, still hesitating over the answer, but the general's purple face and the commissary's cruel smile left very little room for debate. One word too many, and in less time than it would take a rooster to crow he could find himself facing the firing squad, accused of treason.

"That's right… comrade general," he said at last. "It would never occur to me to help an enemy agent in any way."

General Walter half-closed his small, suspicious eyes in search of any trace of insolence in Riley's words, but before he could find any, Merriman seized his arm hard."With your permission, comrade general," he said, "we'll take our leave and let you finish your breakfast. As they say in Spain: *que le aproveche*." He nodded politely and pushed Riley out of the tent in great haste, fearing to hear either of those two hired assassins of Stalin's calling after them.

They did not stop until they reached the Ford, climbed into it in a hurry and urged the driver to start at once and get them away from there. Only then did Merriman snort with relief. Wiping the sweat from his forehead, he turned to Riley, who was sitting beside him in silence."You know what? All through my life I've met a whole bunch of reckless blabbermouths, but you beat all. Do you want to commit suicide? That Commissioner Marty has had hundreds of Republican soldiers shot for much less, and the general has it in for you as well. If you want to get killed, let me know and I'll shoot you myself here and now and save us all the paperwork."

Alex Riley looked somberly out of the window as if he were not listening to Merriman's recriminations. "We're going to lose," he said, so softly the other barely heard him.

"What?" he asked, taken aback.

"You asked me whether I thought we'd win this war," Alex said, turning to his friend. "And that's my answer." He closed his eyes wearily and repeated, "We're going to lose."

7

Back in the camp, with the mid-morning sun threatening another sweltering day, Alex, Jack and Captain Law were sharing a handful of carob pods and a *bota* of watered-down wine in the shade of an olive tree.

Riley had already told them about the incident with the general, and after hearing their well-deserved reproaches and agreeing on how lucky he was that Merriman had been there to get him out of trouble, they were now relaxing in silence, staving off their hunger with those sweet, fleshy fruits which had been used as cattle fodder before the war.

The rest of the company was scattered around, taking up every inch of available shade under the trees. They were all waiting for the order to attack which could arrive any moment, fighting back their fear of dying in the ensuing days with repeated teasing and silly jokes that spread from group to group like gunpowder. Sergeant Fisher even had enough energy to strum the strings of a guitar he had found among the rubble of the village of Quinto.

The soldiers of the Lincoln had composed a song to the music of the ballad *Red River Valley* about the fateful

Battle of Jarama, where hundreds of friends and comrades had lost their life six months back.

*There's a valley in Spain called Jarama
It's a place that we all know so well
It was there that we gave of our manhood
And so many of our brave comrades fell.*

*We are proud of the Lincoln Battalion
And the fight for Madrid that it made
There we fought like true sons of the people
As part of the Fifteenth Brigade.*

*Now we're far from that valley of sorrow
But its memory we ne'er will forget
So before we conclude this reunion
Let us stand for our glorious dead.*

Approximately halfway through the song the slender figure of Martha Gellhorn appeared walking through the groups of men with her striking hair falling loose, wearing sunglasses and men's clothes. She replied with a smile to the whistles of admiration and catcalls which greeted her as she passed, until, shielding her eyes with her hand, she located the trio of officers of the First Company and went straight toward them. "Good morning, gentlemen," she said when she reached them and took shelter in the shade of the olive tree. "I see you got back in one piece, Lieutenant Riley."

"For the moment."

"May I sit down with you?"

"Please do," Law said, and moved aside to make room for her.

"Was last night's patrol profitable?" the journalist wanted to know.

"Quite profitable," Jack replied with the ghost of a smile, rubbing his stomach.

Gellhorn eyed him in puzzlement, but did not ask what he meant. "Anyway, I guess… you can't tell me anything about what you saw."

"You guess correctly, Miss Gellhorn," Law said.

Nevertheless, she turned her full attention on Riley. "I imagined as much. Although, you, lieutenant, owe me an interview," she said. She took off her dark glasses and fixed her blue eyes on him.

"Have you asked my secretary for an appointment? My schedule's very tight."

"I'm sure she'll be able to find a gap for me," she said with a smile.

"If it's up to me," Riley replied with a suggestive wink, "I'll be delighted to find you one."

Ten minutes later they were both strolling beyond the rearguard along a narrow path toward the great carob tree where they had gathered their snack that morning. It was the only shady place in the immediate area, far from the ears and eyes of the rest of the battalion.

Martha Gellhorn had taken out her notebook and was noting down the lieutenant's replies as she walked. Most of the questions so far were personal ones.

"Why would an officer of the Boston Merchant Marine decide to enlist in a war that isn't his own?"

"I've told you that my mother was Spanish."

"That's not reason enough."

"The Nationals shot my maternal grandparents in front of the graveyard wall. Isn't that enough?"

Gellhorn grimaced. Clearly it was not. "What was your life like before you came to Spain?" she asked instead.

"What do you mean?"

"You're not a communist, you had a future in the merchant navy, and I'd bet you weren't short of women to spend time with. I find it hard to believe that you'd leave all that behind to take revenge in some way for the death of your grandparents. Something doesn't fit."

Riley shrugged. "That's your problem."

"Something happened there, didn't it?" she asked, squinting behind her sunglasses. "There's something you're not telling me."

Alex looked at her askance. "There are a lot of things I'm not telling you, Miss Gellhorn."

"I thought we'd agreed you'd call me Martha."

"Okay," he said with a nod. "I don't want to talk about my past any more, Martha."

"And about what happened on the Pingarrón hill, during the Battle of Jarama?"

"Even less."

Finally they reached the shade of the carob tree, and here they stopped.

"I've heard rumors," she insisted as she sat down on the ground beside the trunk. "But I'd like to have your version of the facts."

"And I'd like not to have to talk about it again in my whole life," he replied, making himself comfortable beside her.

"I know you nearly died. I know a bullet missed your heart by barely an inch and that your friend saved you by carrying you to the rearguard under heavy enemy fire. I know you spent many months in hospital recovering, and I know you were promoted to lieutenant."

"Well then, if you know so much about it, why do you ask?"

"Those are the facts, but I want to know the truth," she said, putting aside her notebook. "I want to know the man behind all this. My readers aren't interested in medals or battles, but in Americans who are fighting voluntarily in a foreign country, shoulder to shoulder with soldiers from all around the world, fighting against fascism."

Riley crossed his arms, apparently amused. "Nice speech," he said. "Do you bring it out for everyone you interview so as to loosen their tongues?"

Gellhorn frowned and made a face, but only for a moment.

"To tell you the truth, I do," she admitted finally. "But it hardly ever works."

"That doesn't surprise me. I don't believe that any of those boys" – he waved toward the figures stretched out under the olive trees five hundred yards away – "give a damn about what your readers expect. They just want to be left in peace and not to be asked about the horrors they've had to live through."

"Are you speaking for yourself too?"

"I speak for myself above all."

She was silent for a few seconds, then asked another question. "In that case… if you don't want to talk to me, why did you agree to let me interview you?"

Riley smiled openly, revealing regular white teeth. "I can think of better things to do than wasting our time talking," he said, coming closer to her and slipping his hand around her neck.

"I… it wouldn't be ethical."

"Maybe not," Alex replied, moving close enough to whisper in her ear. "But it'd be fun."

An hour later they were both on their way back to the Lincoln camp, retracing their steps along the path, trying as they went to get rid of the myriad seeds and fragments of dried hay that had caught in their clothes and hair.

Neither said a word, but whenever their eyes met they could not help a conspiratorial chuckle. The glances the rest of the troops turned on their untidy appearance and the murmur that rose as they passed left little doubt as to what it was assumed had gone on between them. And they were right.

"How embarrassing. Oh my God…" Gellhorn muttered, blushing. "It must be written all over our faces."

"Does it worry you?"

"Not particularly. But I wouldn't want them to think I'm a… well, you know what I mean."

"I don't suppose anyone would think you're a… well, you know what I mean."

She punched his shoulder gently. "Don't mock me."

"I'm not. And don't worry, I promise not to give them all the intimate details."

Martha blushed suddenly. "Don't you dare tell them anything!"

"But Martha, please…" He waved toward the troops who were watching them. "That's what would interest my readers."

For a moment she was confused, trying to decide whether he was being serious.

She did not relax until Alex smiled at her, and she sighed in relief. "That wasn't funny," she protested.

"Oh, I think it was."

Gellhorn was about to give him another friendly punch when the baritone voice of Hemingway reached them. "Martha!" he called as he strode toward them. "Where the hell have you—?" He stopped dead and looked at her from head to foot. Her disordered hair full of flecks of straw, her unevenly buttoned blouse, her lips and cheeks lightly reddened…Then he gave Riley the same examination, noticing his malicious smile, and it took him exactly two seconds to form a pretty accurate picture of what had just gone on between the two of them. On the third second he launched himself at Alex with a cry of *Yousonofabitch!* in perfect Spanish.

8

"I just can't believe it," Merriman repeated, shaking his head as he walked around in circles under the green awning which did duty as the Lincoln command post. He stopped in front of the two men and looked them up and down with an air of disappointment.

Hemingway was holding a bloody handkerchief to his nose, one of his shirtsleeves was torn and his glasses were missing a side arm.

Riley, for his part, had a black eye, and his shirt was torn at the front and missing most of its buttons.

"Do you realize what an example of indiscipline you're giving my men?" Merriman spat out. "I ought to throw you out, and as for you, I ought to arrest you!" he told the journalist and the lieutenant, jabbing his finger at them.

"You can't—" Hemingway began.

"What do you mean, I can't?" Merriman burst out. "Throw you out? This is my unit, and I don't give a damn whether it was General Red or the president himself who invited you. I'm the law here. Do you understand?"

Hemingway did not answer, nor did he need to.

"And you," he said, confronting Riley and standing inches away from his face. "I really can't believe you're such a fool. I save you from being arrested this morning, and a few hours later you're in a brawl with this goddamned Ernest Hemingway in front of the whole troop. Don't you have a single trace of common sense?"

"May I answer that?"

"No! You may not! It's a rhetorical question, for god's sake! What am I supposed to do with you, uh? Come on, tell me."

"I—"

"Shut up!"

"Commander Merri—" Hemingway began.

"You shut up too! Both of you shut up and get out of my sight this minute!"

"Yes, sir!" Riley said, saluting and turning to go.

"Okay," Hemingway said, and followed his example.

"Wait a minute!" Merriman shouted, so that both of them turned round once again. "If either of you gives me any more trouble" – he jabbed his finger at them menacingly once again – "I swear to God I'll give you such grief you'll end up begging me to shoot you!"

The two men nodded and resumed their way out toward the ring of onlookers, who had followed the Commander's talking-to from a safe distance and with great interest.

Jack and Gellhorn were waiting at the front, commenting on the two men's unfortunate appearance.

"So how did it go?" Jack asked teasingly.

"Scratch my balls, Jack."

Gellhorn could not help a chuckle, and Hemingway looked at her with wounded pride.

"How could you do this to me, Martha? Getting involved with this moron." He waved disdainfully toward Riley.

"Do this to you, Ernest?" she said. "I can get involved with whoever I feel like. I don't have to justify myself to you."

"How can you say that?" he replied, offended. "What about us?"

Martha Gellhorn crossed her arms in defiance. "Us?" she said, and gave him a steely smile. "Were you thinking of *us* when you slept with that waitress from the Florida Hotel?"

"That was completely different!"

"Sure. Then I had to swallow it, and now it's your turn. Tell me, how does it feel to be humiliated?"

The circle of soldiers had grown in number, and by now more than half the company was assembled around them. A jealous spat between two celebrities was not a show they could expect to watch every day.

"What's going on here, Alex?" Jack asked in Riley's ear.

"I've no idea," he admitted quietly and as shocked as everybody else. "But I'm beginning to get the impression the lady only used me to get her revenge."

His friend nodded understandingly and gave him a comforting pat on the back. "I'm sorry, pal. Really sorry that…"

"Sorry?" Riley cut in, grinning from ear to ear. "What do you mean? The best sex is sex out of spite!"

Luckily the afternoon passed without any other excitement except the arrival of new artillery from Barcelona: a dozen colossal Perm 152 mm howitzers of Soviet manufacture. The first company of the Lincoln had to help set these up and protect them with dirt sacks on the other side of the rise. When those iron beasts started to spit out their ammunition against the rebel positions, the village of Belchite would become a smoking pile of rubble.

Naked from the waist up, Riley and Jack were helping the rest of the men to pile the last sacks into a wall which was not much more than three feet high. Even Captain Law was lending a hand, fully aware that if anything unites men as much as fighting together, it is working together.

"Have they told you when they'll start the bombardment?" Riley asked as he handed him a forty-pound sack of dirt.

"Merriman says…" he said, panting with the effort, "as soon as the planes arrive from Valencia. Maybe even today."

Jack and Riley exchanged a look of concern.

"Although it's late now," he added as he checked the position of the sun, which was already descending toward the horizon. "They probably won't take off until dawn, then get here in the first hour of the morning."

"What about the attack?" Jack asked, taking the sack from the captain's hands. "Do you know when that'll be?"

"I don't think it'll be for another two or three days," Law said. He turned to Alex, ready to be handed another sack.

"In that case," Riley said with a snort, "there won't be any move on our part tonight, right?"

The Afro-American captain straightened abruptly, ignoring the sack Riley was holding and interrupting the chain of work. Frowning suspiciously, he looked at the lieutenant and the sergeant on his left and said, "You two are planning something."

Jack tried to look as if he had no idea what Law was talking about."What? No, No, absolutely not…"

"Aw, come on. I know you as well as if you were my own children. You wouldn't be thinking about disobeying the general's orders, would you?"

"To be honest, the general didn't give us any order," said Riley.

Michael Law's expression darkened when he understood the implications of this."Come with me," he said, stepping out of the line. "Both of you."

Alex and Jack followed their captain obediently until they were out of the hearing of the other soldiers.

Law came to stand in front of the two men and glared at them."So, what exactly is up with you two? Do you want to be shot?"

"Not for the moment, comrade captain," Riley said.

"Cut the crap, Alex. Why? Hundreds of thousands of innocent people have died in this war, and many of them we've killed ourselves. Why are you going to risk your life to save a family of strangers? I swear I don't understand."

"They're not strangers, comrade captain," Riley said. "Last night we gave them our word we'd help them escape."

"Your word?" he repeated as if it were a joke. "Do you really see yourselves as a couple of knights who have to defend their honor? There's no place for promises in this war. We're all soldiers who carry out orders."

"But they're civilians."

"Civilians?" he repeated. "That goddamned village is full of them!"

"We can't save them," Riley said, following his gaze. "But we can save the family we met last night."

"But there are thousands of innocent civilians in Belchite!" Law insisted. He pointed to the bell tower standing out among the ochre roofs. "What difference does it make if one family lives or dies?"

Riley stared at him long and hard."It'll make a difference to them."

The captain of the First Company took a deep breath and raised a finger ready to tell his lieutenant off, but the words never left his lips. Instead he clicked his tongue and studied the two men while he tried to make up his mind whether they were idiots or just plain crazy."I swear I don't understand you," he muttered. "Civilians on both sides die every day. Those people you want to help aren't much different from the ones you've been killing ever since you got to Spain, and if the Nationals find you, or it reaches the general's ears, you'll both be shot."

"We'll try not to let that happen," the Galician said soothingly.

"Don't you even think about being funny with me, Jack. I'm not in the mood."

"I'd never do anything like that, comrade captain."

Law half-closed his eyes, studying the sergeant's face in search of the slightest twitch at the corners of his mouth."You'll be my ruin, the two of you," he said after a while, with a snort. "Do you understand that you're under my direct command, and that if you're found out I'll be blamed too, for allowing it?"

"We know," Riley said with a nod.

"But that's not going to stop you from going ahead with it."

Both of them shook their heads.

"And you understand that if they catch you, I'll swear in front of the general that you disobeyed my orders, and I won't be able to help you in any way."

"Of course."

Law wiped the sweat off his face with a gesture of weariness. "You're crazy as loons. Both of you," he said. There was a long pause before he added, "At ten o'clock on the dot I'll delay the changing of the guard for five minutes, so be ready. It's all I'm going to do for you. Getting back without being noticed is your business. Understood?"

"Many thanks, Michael."

"Don't thank me yet, Alex," the officer said with a frown. "I might change my mind. Oh, and needless to say," he added very seriously, "this conversation never happened."

Jack raised his eyebrows. "What conversation, captain?"

"Be careful, and come back in one piece," the officer finished. "I don't want to have to promote a new lieutenant and find another sergeant before the attack."

"Nobody will even notice we're gone, captain. We'll be back before dawn."

Law nodded without conviction, put his hands behind his back and walked away shaking his head.

Alex and Jack watched the captain on his way back to the rest of the company to help with the last sacks of earth.

"We're going to do it, right?" Jack asked, more to himself than Riley.

"You don't have to come."

"Sure. And you don't have to say stupid things, but you do."

"I mean it. Both of us don't need to go."

"Are we going to have this same argument every single day? I'm coming, period."

Riley turned to his friend. "You know what will happen if anybody lets anything slip."

"Nobody will, *carallo!* You know that better than I do."

"Or we might be picked up. Or in the end the general might be right and those peasants will turn out to be enemy agents, and tonight there'll be a squad of legionnaires waiting for us inside the house."

Joaquín Alcántara crossed his arms and frowned. "Or the Blessed Virgin Mary might appear and make us into nuns," he said in annoyance. "We might kick the bucket any minute of every day, but that isn't going to stop us doing the right thing. You and me. The two of us. Are we clear?"

Riley had known from the beginning that the conversation would end in this way, as it always did, but it was his selfish way of cleansing his conscience. If during their mission or on the way back from it something should happen to his friend, he could convince himself that he had done everything in his power to dissuade him.

On the other hand, Jack also understood the reason for those short-lived arguments which always ended the same way, and he joined in the game. Having been witness to the events in the Battle of Jarama six months back, he could imagine perfectly well the remorse which gnawed at his friend's soul. If those verbal exchanges served to ease Riley's sense of responsibility and in the process let him keep his mind clear and alert, then they were welcome.

Jack sensed that Alex's insistence on saving those civilians had a lot to do with the search for redemption he had noticed in him ever since he had rejoined the brigade after his long convalescence. The disaster of the Pingarrón and the months of rest in hospital had changed him deeply, leaving behind the arrogant, reckless officer he had been and replacing him with someone far warier and more committed.

Riley put his hand on the sergeant's shoulder and smiled gratefully."We're clear."

9

At five to ten at night, Alex and Jack were hiding under cover of the night behind a clump of bushes, waiting for Law to call the sentinel away and so give them those five minutes of promised invisibility.

Officially no one in the company knew what they were going to do, but rumors were inevitable in such a small, idle group of soldiers, and when they left they were followed by silent nods of approval from the men.

Alex Riley checked his watch again, tilting it to see better in the starlight reflected on the hands.

Jack turned his face, covered with black shoe polish, to him. "How much longer?" he whispered.

"It's almost time."

The moment he pronounced those words, the noise of steps on the dry grass reached them from their right, and a crouching silhouette whistled in the dark. "Hey, Francis," it said, "are you there?"

An arm rose from the scrub a dozen yards away.

"Here," replied a low voice. "What's up?"

"The captain wants you to go and see him."

"Now? I'm in the middle of my watch."

"I know, but he told me to come and get you. Look, I'm just the messenger."

The soldier seemed to puzzle over what to do for a moment."Okay," he said, and stood up. "But you're a witness to the fact that I'm coming under orders. I don't want to be held accountable for leaving my post."

"Whatever you want, Francis. But let's go. I don't like it one bit, this standing here in the open."

The silhouettes of the soldiers set off and quickly melted into the darkness that surrounded them.

"It's our turn now," said Riley.

They began to move, crouching, in the opposite direction to the one the two sentinels had taken.

Then an authoritative voice called out behind them, "Stop right zere in ze name of ze Republique!"

They froze, not so much at having been discovered but because of that unmistakable voice, which sounded like a badly-oiled door.

"Turn around!" the man ordered, shining a light on them.

Alex and Jack obeyed without having to be told again, very slowly and with their hands up.

"Well, well, well... what 'ave we got 'ere?" André Marty said. He was obviously pleased about the encounter. "General Walter said it was impossible zat you would dare disobey 'im, zat you could not be so stupid, but I saw the seed of insubordination in your eyes, Lieutenant Riley. I knew you'd betray your comrades and try to 'elp zose fascists escape." He gave a self-satisfied smile. "I knew it." He had his hand on the butt of the gun he carried in his belt. It was an unnecessary gesture, since he was flanked on either side by four men of the general's personal guard, who were pointing 9 mm Schmeiser machineguns at them.

By making them walk through the Lincoln Battalion camp with guns at their backs like two common thieves, Commissioner Marty was flaunting his power over the Americans, whom he considered too individualistic and rebellious, and at the same time sending a warning: anyone who dared defy his authority would suffer the consequences.

Most of the soldiers got to their feet when they saw their comrades being led at gunpoint to Merriman's tent. Hearing those anonymous voices of protest, which grew louder as the sad parade with André Marty at its head passed by, the commander came out straight away. "What's going on here?" he asked in annoyance, addressing Marty. "Why are you taking two of my men prisoners?"

"Oh come on, don't play ze fool, comrade commander," the Frenchman replied, sounding untroubled. "You know perfectly well what is going on."

"I demand an explanation," he insisted with repressed fury, although Riley was not very sure whether it was directed at the commissioner or at himself. "You don't have the authority to arrest them."

The commissioner crossed his arms arrogantly. "Are you sure you want to do zis, comrade commander?" Coming close to the former professor from California, he whispered in his ear, "Do you really want me to show you up by taking away your auzority in front of your men?" He waved at the hundred and more soldiers who were already gathered around them. "Anyzing you may say or do won't stop me from arresting these two traitors, but it might affect your personal situation… dramatically. Do you understand me?"

"I understand you perfectly," Merriman replied in the same tone, "but if you think you can come to my camp and threaten me—"

"I'm not zreatening you," Marty interrupted, stretching his face into a cruel grimace. "I don't zreaten, I don't need to. My auzority is way above yours, and if you get in my way you will be committing a grave failure of discipline, which the comrade general will judge most severely. And in ze end," he added, turning toward Alex and Jack, "zose two will be punished all ze same."

Merriman tried to stay firm, looking disdainfully at the gaunt political commissioner. He was more than a head taller than Marty and could easily break his neck with just one hand. But deep down, he knew all he could do was make a fuss and protest to General Walter, which would be no use at all.

He turned to look at Alex and Jack, in whose eyes he could see the certainty that they would come out of this badly and the knowledge that no one could help them. Merriman was surprised to read a mute *I'm sorry* on Riley's lips.

Marty gave the order to continue and, followed by the two brigadiers and the four soldiers, they walked a few yards away from the camp until they came to the stump of a dead olive tree. There their hands were tied behind their backs and they were made to sit on the ground with their backs against the stump.

"Are you comfortable?" the commissioner asked, taking up his position in front of them with the white row of teeth which made up his smile shining in the dark. "I dare say now you don't zink it's such a good idea to defy auzority!"

"Why don't you go—" the Galician began.

"Jack!" Alex interrupted him. "Shut up!" And lifting his eyes to André Marty's black silhouette, he said, "Comrade commissioner, I declare myself guilty of insubordination, or whatever it is you want to charge me with, but Sergeant Alcántara is innocent. He was just carrying out my orders, and he doesn't have anything to do with any of this. You only need to see his face to realize he's just a fat simpleton with not much brain."

"*Cagüenla!*" Jack protested. "What the hell are you—"

"Goddamn it, Jack, shut up!"

From Marty's throat came a laugh like a hyena's. He seemed to be amused by this exchange."Don't bozer, lieutenant. I know perfectly well 'oo Sergeant Alcántara is, and 'is record of insubordination is almost as long as yours. You are two of a kind, and in a way it makes sense that you should both end up in the same way, *n'est ce pas*?

"And what way would that be?" Jack asked.

The commissioner's teeth glinted once again in the dark."Zat decision will be made by the comrade general… But I'm sure it will be somezing you will not forget for a long time." He gave an abrupt laugh, like a dog with a cough. "And now I shall leave you in full view of your comrades of ze Lincoln, so zat everybody sees ze consequences of your insolence. Tomorrow morning I will come for you and take you to ze general to be judged." He stepped forward and crouched down before the two soldiers."Oh, and let me inform you," he added in confidence, his breath stinking like a garbage can, "zat ze two soldiers I shall be leaving to watch you 'ave orders to shoot if you try to escape. So please" – he laughed again – "do try."

Five minutes later the lights of the political commissioner's car moved away along the dirt path, while two of the men from his personal guard, as he had promised, kept watch on Alex and Jack, guns pointed at them, despite the fact that both of them had their hands tied behind their backs and to the stump of the tree.
"Well, we can't really say this was a surprise." Jack sighed.
"This?"
"The fact that we're under arrest and in a big fucking mess."
"No, to be honest, it isn't."
"Do you think they'll shoot us?"
Riley shook his head."I don't think so. We'll probably be demoted to ordinary soldiers and they'll make us dig latrines for the rest of the war."
"Well, that's a relief, because I was hoping to die in a different way, attacking an enemy trench or destroying a nest of machine guns."
"Seriously?"
Jack cleared his throat and swallowed."Well, not really. I'd much rather kick the bucket in bed between the legs of a beautiful woman, but I'm afraid it's too late for that. I haven't gotten laid in over a year."
"Well, don't look at me."

Jack looked him up and down. "You're not my type," he said. In a different tone of voice he added, "Who do you think could have told Marty? Someone must have."

Riley shrugged, but in the darkness his gesture went unnoticed."Maybe nobody. That thug is a worm, but he's no fool. He might've guessed I was going to disobey him."

"Well, I was thinking of Hemingway, if truth be told. You bedded his girlfriend and he didn't seem to take it too well."

Riley thought for half a second, but dismissed the possibility at once."No, I don't think so. He's not that kind of person. He would rather have challenged me to a boxing match or a duel with pistols. I can't imagine him acting treacherously."

"Well, I wouldn't be so sure."

"You say that because you don't know him."

The sergeant breathed out loudly through his nose before replying."No, Alex. I say it because I can see him coming toward us. To gloat, I guess."

Riley looked up. Picked out against the light of the camp fires, he could clearly see the thickset silhouette of the journalist, who was strolling toward them as if taking a pleasant evening walk.

10

"Evening, comrades," Hemingway greeted the two guards. "How are the prisoners?"

The guards, who had not seen him coming, turned around in surprise with their weapons at the ready.

"Easy," the writer said, raising his hands. "Don't worry, fellas, I've just come to pay them a visit. Don't you know who I am?"

"You're the journalist," one of the soldiers said, in a strong German accent and with equally strong reluctance. "What do you want?"

"Nothing, nothing. I've just come to talk to the prisoners."

"You can't. Go away."

"It'll only be a minute."

"Nobody can come near the prisoners," the other soldier put in. This one had a Slavic accent, and his tone was less aggressive. "Comrade commissioner's orders."

"But I'm not just anybody," he objected. "I'm Ernest Hemingway, a personal friend of General Vicente Rojo, with a free pass to go anywhere I wish and speak to whoever I want. Do you really believe Commissary Marty's orders are above those of the general in command of the Republican Army?"

The guards hesitated, and Hemingway took that moment to put his hand in his pocket and take out a small hip flask, which he offered to the two guards. "Want some? It's good whisky."

"We can't drink while we're on duty," said the one with the Slavic accent.

"Who's going to tell?" He pointed to Alex and Jack and added, "These two?"

"We can't drink," the German one repeated. "So put that away."

"Okay… I just meant to be friendly," he said apologetically. He took a sip, then put the flask back in his pocket. "And a cigarette? You are allowed to smoke, aren't you?"

"We have our own tobacco," countered the Slav, patting his pocket.

"Do you mean that awful Russian muck you smoke? Those aren't cigarettes, they're pure poison. Would you like to try a real American cigarette?"

This time the guards exchanged glances, then stretched their hands out to the writer.

Hemingway took an opened packet of Camels out of his shirt pocket and offered each of them a cigarette.

The soldiers took them eagerly and put them to their lips at once.

"Wait…" Hemingway said, reaching toward the seat of his pants. "I think I have a lighter somewhere."

They came closer, holding their cigarettes in their mouths to get a light, but what they met was the barrel of a

45 Colt gun in their faces and the unmistakable click of the safety catch.

"Leave your guns on the ground," Hemingway ordered them, casting aside the friendly tone he had used until then. "Very slowly."

It took the two sentinels a moment longer to emerge from their stupefaction and realize what was happening.

"We won't," the German said defiantly. "What are you going to do? Shoot us?"

"I'd rather not get to that point, but I will if you don't give me any other choice."

"They'll execute you."

"No way," he said sounding amused. "At most they'll throw me out of the country. It's one of the advantages of being a celebrity, no one will dare touch me. And take your hands off the machinegun unless you're willing to put me to the test," he added almost kindly. "Drop your weapons and nobody will get hurt."

"If we do that," the Slav said, "then the commissioner will have us executed."

"It's possible, but you can put all the blame on me and you're sure to go free. Otherwise I'll shoot you both before you can even think about pulling the trigger, and you won't be able to smoke any more cigarettes. What do you say? Is it worth the risk?"

"You won't shoot us in cold blood," the German said.

"Are you sure?" Hemingway replied.

There followed a few seconds of tension which seemed an eternity, and finally there came the thud of a gun hitting the ground, followed immediately by another.

Three minutes later, the guards were in Alex and Jack's place, tied to the stump and gagged. The two soldiers gave the knots a final check and moved the machineguns to one side.

In the inadequate starlight, Hemingway and Riley faced each other.

"Thanks," Alex said, offering his hand. "I don't know why you've done it, but thank you."

The writer shook his hand vigorously. "I can't stand bullies, that's all."

"I thought journalists just observed and documented the blood of others."

"Not all journalists are the same. Just as not all soldiers are the same."

"Excuse me if I interrupt," Jack cut in. "But I'm not sure our situation has got any better. The opposite, if anything."

"What do you mean?" Alex asked.

"Well, a moment ago we were under arrest, pending a trial that would hardly have meant we'd be executed. Now, on the other hand" – he waved at the two bound and gagged soldiers – "it's going to be pretty hard to avoid the firing squad."

Hemingway took off his beret and scratched his head. "I did this so you could escape," he said. "It won't be hard for you to reach the French border from here, or board a ship in Barcelona or Valencia to take you out of the country."

Alex Riley shook his head. "I'm not running away. After all I've been through in this war... no, I'm not deserting."

"In that case… what are you going to do?"

Riley took a deep breath, and then gave his answer. "I'm going to help that peasant family to cross the lines, like I promised."

"Are you serious?" Hemingway stared at Alex in disbelief. "But… after all that's happened, you're still thinking of helping them?"

"Of course, even more than before. If they're going to shoot me, then at least it'll have been worthwhile."

"Maybe," Jack said thoughtfully, "there's a third possibility that wouldn't mean either desertion or death."

Both Riley and the journalist turned to him. He was slowly stroking his thick week-old beard.

"And suppose we go and help those people… but then come back before dawn and behave as if nothing had happened?"

Alex looked at him in bafflement. "As if nothing had happened?" He gestured at the two sentinels, who were staring at them wide-eyed. "I'd say it's a bit too late for that, Jack."

"It doesn't have to be," Jack said with a sly grin. "These two are in a fix almost as bad as ours because they let us go. They're the ones most concerned that Marty shouldn't find out about tonight's business. So… if we come back before dawn, we untie our two friends and take their place, and nobody needs to be any the wiser about what happened tonight."

Hemingway nodded in admiration. "You're a smart guy, Sergeant Alcántara. Although we'd have to be sure that these two are ready to cooperate."

"That's easy to find out," said Riley. He crouched down beside the two soldiers. "Okay," he said, "you've heard everything, so I don't need to ask you. What d'you say?"

The writer offered to keep watch on the two sentinels, whom they kept gagged to make sure they did not change their minds in the middle of the night. Meanwhile Alex and Jack slipped away along the edges of the camp, where scarcely anybody was still awake, and after a long detour they reached the ditch they had used the previous night. Hastily, but without abandoning caution, they went along it until the farm came into sight.

"Can you see anything?" Jack asked Riley, who had put his head up to see above the edge.

"Just like yesterday. Everything's dark."

"That's a good sign."

"I guess."

"You didn't really mean what you said before, that it might be a cunning trap by the Nationals, did you?"

Alex took a moment to reply. "No. Of course not." As he moved on he added, "But it wouldn't hurt to be careful for once."

After a couple of minutes they reached the back of the house, exactly as they had the day before, and in the same way they climbed out of the ditch and went stealthily up to the wall.

The gun he carried at the back of his trousers was sticking into Riley's lower back. It was the one the journalist had used to subdue the guards and which turned out to be his own old 45 Colt. He had not asked Hemingway how he had managed to take it away from Merriman, who was the one Marty had given it to after arresting them.

Holding their breath and straining their ears, they waited a few moments without moving, but not a single sound came from the house.

Following the same route as the previous day, they went around the house until they reached the north window. This time they found it had been closed from the inside, so that they had no choice but to go to the entrance, a small door made of rough-hewn boards clumsily nailed together.

"Señor López…" Alex called through the door, using his hands to muffle the sound. "Señor López…"

Silence.

"They should be waiting for us, right?" Jack wondered aloud.

"Eustaquio…" Riley insisted. "Are you there? It's Joaquín and Alex."

Nothing.

"This is very weird," Jack said. "We ought to…"As he spoke he leaned on the rough door, which opened with a creak under the weight of his hand.

The inside of the house, dark as a cavern, gave them no clue as to what might be waiting for them.

"Hello?" Riley said, poking his head in. "Anybody there?"

No answer came from inside.

"*Cagüenla*," Jack grunted, "there's nobody here. We're risking our necks, so—"

Alex put his hand on the other's chest."Shhh… quiet…"

"What?"

"I think I heard something."

"My stomach, probably. I barely had any dinner."

Alex looked at him reproachfully. "You had yours and half of mine," he reminded him. "And the sound came from inside the house."

"Well then, it'll be rats. It's clear there's nobody in here."

Riley strained his eyes, trying to pierce the darkness. "Most probably. But now we're here, we'd better make sure."

Carefully he crossed the threshold, followed closely by Jack. As soon as they had closed the door behind them Alex took out the lighter Hemingway had given him and held it up to illuminate the room.

The faint orange light of the flame barely lit up more than a few yards, but it was enough to make it clear that something had happened there. Something bad. All the furniture had been thrown haphazardly around the floor, even the heavy wooden table, and fragments of clay bowls and glassware covered the floor and crunched under their footsteps.

"Shit," said Jack, summing up the situation perfectly.

Alex picked up an oil lamp, miraculously intact, and lit it. The extent of the break-in became apparent. "There are no bodies. Nor blood," he said, relieved. "They must have taken them."

"The Nationals," Jack added unnecessarily.

"Who else? They must have found out they were planning to escape and taken them back to the village."

"Motherfuckers… what did they care? Why stop them?"

"If their commanders are half as paranoid as ours," Riley said, "they'll have accused them of being communist spies, or something of the sort."

Jack's face suddenly took on a worried look. "Could they have told them... we were coming?" he asked, knowing the answer in advance.

Alex tensed, realizing the implications of this. "We've got to leave right now," he said, putting out the oil lamp and heading to the door. But he stopped dead with his hand already on the latch and raised his head like a hunting dog. "It's not rats," he said in warning as he turned around. He took out the lighter again, and keeping it alight he crept to one of the doors at the end, opened it and found what must have been the bedroom shared by Eustaquio and his wife.

To one side was an old closet, its doors wide open, the clothes all strewn at their feet, as if it had been gutted. On the far end a wooden crucifix hung on the whitewashed wall, and underneath it on the upset bed was a mattress shedding straw through its open seams.

Riley went to the middle of the room, looked to left and right, and very slowly knelt down. He put the lighter on the floor, lowered his head until his cheek touched the cold stone, and peered under the bed.

From the shadows a pair of eyes was watching him in terror.

11

Joaquín Alcántara came back from the pantry with a jug and three glasses and laid them on the table Alex had put back up. He sat down and filled them halfway with the same strong red wine they had drunk the night before, under very different circumstances.

Facing the two soldiers, his dirty face showing the marks the tears had left and his eyes restless, Javier was sitting in one of the chairs with his chin on the edge of the table.

Jack handed the boy one of the glasses, which he took with both hands.

"Mother only lets me drink a little," Javier said with his nose inside the glass.

"Today's a special day," said Jack. "Drink it all."

Riley turned to his friend. "Are you sure?"

"It'll settle his nerves," he explained. "My father gave it to me when I was little, and you can see how well I turned out."

Riley stared at his friend, trying to guess whether he was serious or not. He finally decided it was not important."Right then, Javier," he said, turning to the boy, "you say the soldiers took your parents, your sisters, your grandparents and your uncles and aunts."

The little boy shook his head. "No," he said. He sounded bored, as if he were repeating the story for the umpteenth time. "They took my parents and my little sisters. They caught my uncles, my aunts, my cousins and my grandparents when they were leaving the village."

"Did you see them?"

"Yes, I saw them. And I ran home to tell my father, but then they came here too."

"And you hid under the bed," Jack concluded.

"Mother told me to. I didn't want to. But she told me to stay until you came."

"Is that what she said?"

Javier nodded vigorously and added "And to go with you a long way away from the village, and never come back. But I don't want to go alone. I want to go with my mamma and papa. Will you take me with them?"

Jack swallowed and leaned on the table. "You see, Javier, we…" He cleared his throat awkwardly. "Right now we can't take you to your parents. They're—"

"Why not?"

"Well… because…" He glanced to his left. "Help me out, Alex."

The lieutenant glanced at him in annoyance, but put his glass aside and explained, "Your parents have been arrested by our enemies, so we can't go to the village. Do you understand? Besides, we don't know where they are."

"Yes."

"Yes, you understand?"

"Yes, I know where they are."

"You do?"

89

"Sure. In the church. I heard one of the soldiers say so. Will you take me with them?" the boy insisted.

"We can't, Javier. We have to leave, and you're coming with us like your mother told you."

"But I don't want to go." He was on the verge of tears. "I want to go with them."

"Sorry, son, that's not possible."

"Yes, it is!" he shouted furiously. "I can go by myself! I know the way!" He slammed the glass on the table and got to his feet.

"Stop right there, lad," Jack said sternly. "Sit down." He waited for the boy to obey, and added, "It's very dangerous to go to the village, and as from tomorrow they're going to start dropping bombs on it, so if you go you'll get killed. And your mother wouldn't want you to get killed, would she?"

The boy shook his head slowly, but then frowned and asked, "But all my family are there… what's going to happen to them?" He began to sob miserably. "Are they going to die? I don't want them to die!"

"No. They're not going to die. They—"

"Yes, they are!" He pointed an accusing finger. "You just said so!"

Riley sat back in his chair and folded his arms. "Very good, Jack," he murmured. "I see you know how to handle children."

"Stop crying, Javier," Jack said, but the boy was not listening any more.

"I don't want them to die! You must save them! Father said you were going to save us!"

"That's not—"

"You said it!" he cried amid sobs. "If you hadn't come here last night, they wouldn't have taken my parents! It's all your fault!"

"No, Javier. That's not true."

To Jack's surprise, it was his friend who replied, "Yes, it is."

"What?"

"He's right, it's our fault." He breathed deeply and blew all the air out at once. "We're the ones who caused all this." He leaned his elbows on the table and buried his face in his hands. "We're to blame."

Jack half-closed his eyes suspiciously before he asked, "Where are you going with this?"

Riley lifted his head with a stoical grimace. "You know."

"You've got to be kidding me."

"I'm absolutely serious."

"But—"

"I know all the buts, Jack," he said, and put his hand on his friend's shoulder. "But I have to do it."

Jack rubbed the back of his neck, and with the resignation of a condemned man he said, "*We* have to."

"Are you sure?"

"Course I'm not." He smiled sadly. "But for once, it would be nice to do some good in this fucking war."

"That's the idea," Riley agreed with a nod. Then he turned to the boy. Until then he had not realized he had stopped crying and was staring at them with eyes like saucers.

"Are you going to get my parents?"

"We are."

The boy jumped over the table and threw himself at Riley, hugging him as a castaway would a log. Then he let go and did the same with Joaquín, repeating into his ear over and over, "Thank you, thank you, thank you."

When Javier had calmed down and Jack had discreetly wiped away a couple of tears they started to work out the unlikely rescue plan.

They spread a half-scribbled piece of paper on the table. On it Riley drew a rough map of Belchite with the stub of a pencil according to the boy's instructions and the little he could remember from the map the general had showed them the day before.

The village, as drawn in the light of the oil lamp, showed an irregular potato shape, slightly longer from east to west. The López's farm, where they were, was half a mile or so to the north. As a representation, of course, it left a lot to be desired, but it was better than nothing.

"Right, then," said Riley, resting the tip of the pencil stub on the Convent of San Agustín. "So we have the convent here, and you say you heard them say they were taking your parents to the church, which is…"

"Here," Javier said, putting his finger on the piece of paper.

"And the command center?" Jack asked.

"The what?"

"The headquarters," he corrected himself. "The building where the generals are. With flags and soldiers at the door."

"Ah, that's here," he said happily, stabbing his finger again. "Right beside the church."

"Wonderful," said Jack, making a face.

"Do you remember if there were many soldiers?" Riley asked.

The boy shook his hand, raised his eyebrows and exclaimed, "A whole crowd! More than there are people in the village!"

Alex and Jack exchanged a look that needed no words.

It was all looking worse every minute.

Riley put the pencil on the table and leaned back in his chair. He fixed his gaze on the ceiling and tried to imagine some way of getting to the church without being seen. How to get out of there with civilians in tow, some of them children and elderly people, was something he did not even dare think about. He turned to the boy, realizing he had not asked a crucial question. "Javier, do you know how many of your family the soldiers took?"

The boy nodded. Raising the tips of his fingers to his lips, he began to recite, very seriously, "One. Two. Three. Seven. Fourteen. Nine. Fifty. Twenty. Sixteen…"

Jack rolled his eyes, and Riley nearly burst out laughing at the absurdity of the whole situation."Okay, okay… and with your fingers? Can you show me how many there were on your fingers?"

Once again Javier thought hard and started to raise the fingers of his right hand one by one, and when there were no more left he started on the left hand. And then again with those of the right hand.

"That's fifteen people!" cried Jack.

"Don't know," the boy said nonchalantly.

"Are you sure it's as many as that, Javier?" Riley asked.

Javier nodded decidedly.

"Okay… let's say there are fifteen of them" – he looked at Joaquín – "and at least half of them will be children and old folks. What do you think?"

"Do you really want to know what I think?"

"No. Not really."

"I guessed as much." He stretched his lips in a grin. "We don't even know how to get into the village without being caught."

"That's right. They must be keeping a permanent watch on the field around the village, which to top it all doesn't offer us a single goddamned tree to hide behind." Turning his attention to Javier once again, he asked, "You wouldn't know of a way to get into the village without being seen, would you?"

The boy looked at him as if he had just been asked whether he could kick a ball. "Of course," he answered. His voice sounded almost offended. "Along the big ditch."

"Are you serious?" Jack asked.

"Of course," he said again. "It's the way I've been going in and out ever since the soldiers came."

"And… where is this ditch?"

"Behind the house." He pointed behind him. "It's the one that comes from Codo and gets as far as the village, in front of the convent."

Riley picked up the pencil stub and began to trace a line from the farm to the oil factory, beside the abandoned Convent of San Agustín.

"This way?" he asked, indicating the map. "This is the way the ditch goes?"

Javier nodded confidently. "Now it's dry," he said rather sadly, "because it hasn't rained in more than a month. When there's water in it I go there with my cousins to bathe."

Riley looked at his friend again, his grimace giving way to a sly smile. "We have our point of entry," he said. He sounded almost elated. "Do you feel like taking a walk?"

Jack stood up with a similar look on his face. "I thought you'd never ask."

12

The big ditch was not completely dry, as the boy had described it. A thread of water trickled along the bottom, and the ground the two soldiers trod was covered by a film of evil-smelling mud which stuck to the soles of their boots like gruel. What with that and the discomfort of walking bent double for more than half a mile, their route along the ditch seemed to take an eternity.

"We're almost there," whispered Riley, half-turning as he spoke.

"About time," Jack replied in the same tone. "By the way, what time is it?"

Riley looked at his watch, turning it this way and that so that the starlight would shine on the hands. "Twenty past one."

"*Carallo*," said Jack. "We've wasted more than three hours."

"Dawn's at half past seven. We still have six hours."

"It'll be a close call."

"I know. Come on."

They kept walking, bent double, heading for the Convent of San Agustín, which by now was not far away.

The windows of the factory were black rectangles which stood out in the brick façade, like holes in a set of dentures. Although there seemed to be nobody inside the building, Riley had no doubt that enemy soldiers would be keeping watch inside it behind those windows, under cover of darkness.

With extreme caution they went on along the ditch until they came to a small wall, right in front of the factory wall itself. This gave them extra protection and the chance to lean against it and rest for a moment, out of sight of the sentinels.

Jack rested his back against the low wall beside Riley. "I was afraid there'd be booby traps or some kind of alarm in the ditch, and we'd make them go off as we passed," he whispered.

"Is that why you insisted I go first?"

"Your eyes are better than mine. And so is your luck."

"At least you could've warned me."

Jack smiled innocently. "I didn't want to scare you."

"How kind of you…" Riley said feigning disappointment. "At least it seems the rebels weren't counting on anybody sneaking into the village."

"Anybody stupid enough, you mean. And speaking of which… I don't seem to see anybody looking out of the windows. Do you think they could be so careless as not to keep any watch?"

"I haven't seen anybody either, but there's sure to be someone in hiding. I'd stake my pay on it."

"What pay?"

"Just saying. Let's go on." He nodded to the east. "We still have to get to the other side of the village."

They followed the winding line of the wall, walking very slowly with their heads down, stopping every time they heard the slightest noise, until they reached the façade of the abandoned convent which towered above as the tallest building in Belchite.

Immediately in front of them a section of the wall several yards long had crumbled. If they went past it they would be visible to anybody watching.

"What do we do?" Jack whispered at Riley's back. "Can you see anything?"

Alex poked his head very carefully through the gap, taking a good look at the convent's great open windows, but all he could see was absolute darkness. From where they were he could barely see the four windows right in front of them, but if he leaned further out he risked being seen.

Although there seemed to be nobody there.

He waited almost a minute for any noise or movement which might give away the presence of a sentinel, but nothing happened. However incredible it might seem, apparently the place was empty.

Nevertheless, they could not stay there indefinitely, so he clenched his teeth and prepared to cross the unprotected space.

Riley was just taking his first step when a gust of wind wafted the unmistakable smell of tobacco to him. He stopped and stood absolutely still, staring into the darkness behind the windows once again, and he could see that in one of them there shone the tiny glow of a cigarette.

"What do we do?" Jack whispered. "It's the only way in, and we can't go around it."

"We'd have to distract the man. Or men. There could be more of them."

"How?"

"Make them look the other way for a few seconds."

"Again, how?"

"I don't know. Well…" he hesitated, "maybe I do. It occurs to me I might be able to make some kind of smoke bomb."

His friend frowned. "You're joking."

"No, seriously. I read it in the Brigade Manual."

"Is there a Brigade Manual?"

"Of course there… Bah, it doesn't matter. What's interesting is that it tells you how to make a smoke bomb with a little shoe polish, a sock, some gunpowder and dry grass." He took out his lighter and gun and added, "And we have all the components."

"Yeah. And you know how to make it?"

"I can try."

Jack shook his head, not at all convinced. "I don't like it. If it doesn't work, you'll start a fire and then they really will see us."

"Yeah… you might be right," Riley admitted. "But I can't think of anything else."

"Well, look here… I can." He moved about twenty yards away in the direction they had come from and searched among the weeds. After a moment he straightened up, weighing something in his hand.

Alex had a sudden ominous feeling about what his friend intended to do, and had to keep back a shout. He hurried toward him, waving his arms, but Jack either did not see him or did not want to.

Gathering momentum, Jack slung his arm back and hurled a huge rock over the low wall against one of the few windows in the convent that still had glass in it.

The sharp noise of shattering glass was like the crack of lightning breaking the silence of the night. It seemed to Riley that the noise must have been audible in every corner of Belchite, as if a bomb had fallen in the middle of the village. Struck dumb by Jack's stupidity, he stared, motionless, expecting bullets to rain down on them any minute.

As soon as he had thrown the rock, Jack hastened back."Come on, let's go," he said. "Don't just stand there like a stuffed dummy."

Riley blinked in puzzlement, groping for words to express his disagreement with what Jack had just done, but he realized his friend had gone past him, peered out of the hole in the wall and slipped through it without anybody shooting at him or raising the alarm."Son of a…" he swore in a whisper. Not bothering to look first, he ran after Jack who was waiting on the other side with his arms crossed and a look of satisfaction on his face.

After the short sprint Riley reached his side with his heart in his mouth, more because of the tension than the effort. As he leaned against the wall he heard Jack say proudly, "Sometimes the simplest plans are the best ones."

Luckily they did not find any more gaps in the wall, and the voices of the guards, intrigued by the shattered glass, were left behind.

Riley was still thinking about Jack's crazy stunt and their incredible luck that nobody had seen them when they reached the end of the wall. Here it merged with the façades of the houses on the outer rim of the town center. They stopped for a moment to check that there was no one in sight. Then, bent double so that they were almost on all fours, they went into a narrow cobbled alley which led to the village, flanked by well-constructed two- and three-story buildings.

Every few steps they stopped to listen, always looking for shelter in the shadows of arches and doors. The street, like all those in Belchite, was completely dark, nor was there the faintest trace of light from the windows. Apparently the occupying forces had decreed a curfew and forbidden any kind of lighting at night.

In this way they came to a small triangular plaza where no less than seven streets met. Alex looked up, and in spite of the darkness he was able to make out the plaque with the sign *Plaza de San Salvador*. This plaza did not appear in the rough map he was carrying in his pocket.

"So what now?" Jack whispered in his ear, thinking of the seven streets in front of them. "Where to?"

Riley shrugged. "I've no idea," he admitted. "But I think it must be one of those." He indicated two of the streets which started right ahead of them. One was noticeably wider than the other.

"I vote for the narrow one," Jack said. "It's darker."

"That's true. But the other one seems to go right—" Before he could finish the sentence they heard the faint sound of footsteps and voices coming toward them.

"A patrol," muttered Jack forcefully, gesturing at the wide street the sound was approaching from.

"Down the other, down the other," Alex urged in a whisper, and hurried across the plaza silently. "Come on!"

They were slipping into the blackness of the alley when two Moorish soldiers came into the plaza and stopped. From the relative safety of the shadows, they watched as the two Moroccans leaned their Mausers against the wall and proceeded to smoke nonchalantly, unaware of the presence of the two enemy soldiers.

"We only just made it," Jack gasped.

Riley nodded in agreement. Patting him on the shoulder, he urged him on.

This street was even narrower than the one before, and over their heads the balconies of the buildings almost touched the ones opposite. Riley looked up and thought that two neighbors looking out of the window at the same time could easily shake hands without needing to leave their homes.

A hundred yards or so ahead the alley opened up as it joined another street, and finally they saw the hexagonal bell tower of the church in front of them, outlined against the starry sky.

"The church," Riley announced with a smile. "And it's not being watched. I think we're in luck."

Jack pointed to the right. "I'd wait before I cracked open the champagne."

Intrigued, Riley looked in the direction his friend was pointing in, and his heart sank to his feet.

Fifty yards or so to their right, on the other side of a rectangular plaza flanked by fragile saplings, rose the wall of another church. It was very similar in shape and size to the one in front of them.

"Another church?" He groaned. "The kid didn't tell us there were two churches."

"And that's not the worst of it. Take a careful look."

Riley strained his eyes to see through the heavy shadows that enveloped the plaza.

He could see nothing at first except a military truck and a machinegun set up behind some bags of earth, but after a moment something moved at the limits of his perception and he glimpsed several silhouettes posted behind those bags, a few yards from the church door. "Soldiers," he muttered under his breath.

"There's half a dozen of them," said Jack. He crouched down beside Riley. "Not counting those we can't see. There's no way we can get any nearer without being seen."

Alex nodded silently in agreement.

Then they heard the muffled sound of laughter.

They turned around at once, exchanging worried glances.

It seemed that the patrol they had left behind had taken the same route as themselves and would soon appear around the corner of the narrow alley.

They could not stay where they were, nor go back, and if they went out into the plaza they would be seen immediately.

There was no escape route.

13

Riley grabbed Jack's arm and urged him to move. "To the church," he whispered, and dragged him toward the door in front of them.

In two strides they were facing the solid wooden door, which inevitably was closed. Trying hard not to make any noise, they leaned their whole weight against it, but it did not budge an inch.

"*Cagüenla.* It's locked from the inside." Jack groaned.

Alex pushed once again, but gave up, realizing it was impossible. They could not get into the church, and the footsteps were coming closer.

A recurring feeling of fatalism came over Alex. As Jack went on uselessly pushing the door, he reached for the gun at his back.

They had nowhere to hide, so that the only thing left for them to do was to surprise the approaching soldiers and try to escape from the village, taking advantage of the confusion. But he was aware that once the alarm was raised, the chances of getting away alive were very…

Suddenly, his eyes became conscious of a point six feet above his head, but it took his brain an instant longer to process what he was seeing.

An open window.

"Jack!" He raised his voice more than he should have. "Look."

His friend looked up and saw what Riley had seen.

"Come on," he urged, went to stand by the wall, and made a stirrup with his hands to boost Jack. "Get up!"

"But…"

"No buts! Climb onto my shoulders."

Jack blinked in indecision. Finally he clambered on Riley's back, who shook with the effort of supporting his heavily-built weight.

"For God's sake, get up!" Riley gasped.

"I still can't reach the window…" Jack muttered, trying to get his foot into a gap in the stone wall. At last, holding fast to the windowsill, he managed to get in.

The voices of the sentinels were perfectly audible now. Alex calculated that he had less than twenty seconds to reach the window Jack had already disappeared through.

He pushed himself up and grasped a pipe fixed to the wall. Using it as a sort of liana, he climbed up until he reached the level of the window, which was about eighteen inches to his left. At that point he followed Jack's example, putting the toe of his boot in a small hollow in the wall and reaching for the windowsill. But just when he was about to jump he lost his footing and suddenly found himself hanging from the window with one hand and both feet in the air.

A new burst of laughter sounded to his left, and when he turned he saw the tip of one of the soldiers' cigarettes shining in the dark. He was aware that they might as well be able to see a five-foot-eleven man hanging like a monkey from the façade. He tried to heave himself up, but with no foothold it was impossible. Clenching his teeth, he made one last effort before it was too late, and when his strength was beginning to fail and he feared he would crash down into the middle of the street, two powerful hands grasped his wrists and pulled him up as if he were nothing more than a rag doll.

When his feet crossed the window he accidentally hit the jamb, making a dull noise. The soldiers, who were at that moment almost beneath, looked up. Luckily, an instant after the heel of his boot had disappeared from sight.

They stayed completely still, dreading to hear a voice sounding the alarm or someone knocking on the house door to investigate. But after a few seconds of uncertainty, holding their breaths, they heard one of the soldiers say something apparently funny in Arabic and then the other laughing as they went away.

Only then did Jack and Alex drop to the floor, gasping, exhausted by the tension and the effort.

"That was close," Jack said. "We only just made it."

"Starting tomorrow..." Alex said, panting, "you go on a diet."

As soon as they got their breath back, they stood up and by the dim light coming in through the window tried to find out where they were.

They were not in a bedroom but in some kind of studio with a large oak table in the middle, scattered with papers and dominated by an oversized crucifix.

"What now?" Jack asked. "Do we go back down to the street?"

"What for? We can't get into the church beside here, and the other's being watched so we can't get in there either."

Jack seemed to weigh up his next words before he spoke. "Right, so…we go back?"

"No. Not yet. Not till we're sure there's nothing else we can do."

"Okay, but what if they have them in one of the churches, but we can't get into either one of them?"

"I don't know, Jack. But I think we ought to take a look." He pointed at the table. "That crucifix, and the fact that the house is wall-to-wall with the church, might mean something. You never know. Maybe this is the priest's quarters, and it might have a back door, or even a passage that communicates with the church."

Jack shrugged, not too optimistically. "Well, now we've gotten to the river," he said philosophically, "let's try to cross the bridge."

"Exactly." Alex slapped Jack's shoulder. He went across to the door, grasped the knob and turned to his friend. "Ready?"

"No," he admitted. "But I'll never be any more ready than this."

Riley turned the knob and opened the door ready to go through. Inches away from his own face there materialized the astonished face of a heavy-set woman of about sixty. In her left hand she was holding a lighted candelabra and in her right a poker. She wore a white habit and a black wimple that covered her from head to toe.

"What on earth—" the woman began as soon as she had recovered from her surprise. But she was not able to finish the question.

Alex covered her mouth with one hand, while dragging her with brute force into the studio. Jack closed the door behind them.

Sitting in a chair in the light of the candelabra, the nun glared at the two soldiers.

Jack was just closing the window shutters, while Alex, who still had his hand over the nun's mouth, said, "We're not going to hurt you. I just want to ask you a few questions and then we'll leave." With a warning gesture he added, "So don't scream, and nobody will get hurt."

He took his hand away. No sooner had he done this than the nun cried out, "Get out of—"

Instantly Riley covered her mouth again with his left hand, while with his right he drew the Colt from the back of his pants and held it in front of the nun's face for her to see it clearly."You don't think I'm serious?" he asked threateningly, and moved closer to her face. "If you raise your voice again, I swear by your God I'll shoot you. Do you understand? Nod if you do."

The nun looked into Riley's eyes and nodded, very slowly.

"Right," he said, and drew his hand back a few inches. "Let's try again. What's your name?"

The tightened lips of the woman seemed to be holding back a rebuff, and they still took a while to open again."Who are you?" she asked with controlled fury.

"We ask the questions here," Riley rapped out. "I'll say it once more." He raised the gun once again. "What's your name?"

"Do you think you're going to scare me with your little gun?" the nun said defiantly. "If you shoot, the whole village will hear it, and in a minute this room will be full of soldiers who—"

Before she could finish the sentence, Jack crouched in front of her and unsheathed the knife of one of the watchmen they had gagged and tied up."You were saying?"

"This is the house of God…" she protested, rather less confidently. "You have no right to come in here. There's nothing for you to take."

"We're not here to rob you," Riley said.

The nun's face, far from being reassured, showed sudden alarm."So what have you come for, then?" she asked. Now she sounded really worried. "I warn you, if you try to take advantage of me, the wrath of God will—"

"Relax, grandma," Jack said. He twisted his mouth into a smile and put the knife back in its sheath. "I have no intention of touching even one hair of your head. I'm not that desperate."

"Tell us your name and what this place is," Riley demanded.

The nun looked at him in puzzlement."This is the Convent of San Rafael, naturally."

"And you are…?"

She introduced herself at last. "Sister Divine Charity, Mother Superior of the Dominican Sisters of Belchite."

"Okay, sister. This is Sergeant Alcántara, and I'm Lieutenant Riley, of the International Brigades."

Hearing this, the nun crouched back in the chair with horror on her face, as if she had just seen the devil himself."Reds!" she cried.

Riley was obliged to cover her mouth once again."Don't raise your voice," he said firmly. "We don't want to hurt you. I just want some information. Is that clear?"

The nun's proud gaze had turned to pure terror, and for a moment Alex thought of the atrocities some other soldiers must have committed on other nuns to create such an extreme reaction. Of course the fact that they were dressed in black, with their faces blackened, and had come in through the window in the middle of the night surely did nothing to help.

"Calm down," he insisted. With a smile that was meant to be reassuring, he put the gun away. "All we want to know is whether there's any way to get from here to the church without having to go out in the street." He withdrew his hand and added in a whisper, "Please don't scream."

The nun seemed to relax a little, just enough to be able to speak again."The church? You want to go into the church? Why? Do you want to steal the images? Have you no respe—"

"I've already told you we're not thieves," Jack cut in, his patience nearly at its end. "We've come to set free some villagers the Nationals have arrested and, we think, locked up in the church."

Riley looked at his sergeant out of the corner of his eye. He did not want the nun to know about their intentions. Not yet, at least.

"Some villagers locked up in the church?" she asked, with sincere surprise. "What sort of story is this? There's nobody locked up in my church."

"And in the other one?" Alex asked. He pointed to the window. "We've noticed there's another one on the other side of the plaza."

"San Martín de Tours?" she asked in surprise. "Why would they lock anybody in there? That's what the headquarters is there for."

"It might be because there are too many people, and there wasn't room in the cells. Who knows? The point is, we have reason to believe they're being held prisoner there."

"Well, if they've been taken there'll be some reason for it," the nun said. She had regained her haughtiness. "They'll be reds too, she said disdainfully. "Serves them right!"

"You bloody—"

"Sergeant!" Riley interrupted him, putting his hand on his chest. Turning back to the nun, he muttered under his breath, "Sometimes I forget why I'm fighting in this war, Sister Charity, but people like you always help me remember."

14

"I'm not saying anything," the mother superior repeated. She folded her arms. "You can do whatever you want to me, but I'm not going to help you."

"That's what you'd like us to do, you old witch," Jack said.

"Jack… you're not helping," Riley said. Then, to the nun, "I'm just asking you to tell us how to get to the church without being seen. Then we'll leave the same way we came."

Jack cleared his throat and looked in the direction of the window.

"So to speak," Riley added. "Believe me, we don't want to hurt you, Sister Charity, just to find those people and leave the village before sunrise."

"No chance of that," the nun insisted arrogantly.

Riley exchanged an eloquent look with his sergeant, who gave an understanding nod. "Okay," he said and tore away the curtain cord with a jerk. "Jack, gag her."

Jack took a dirty handkerchief out of his pocket and tied it over the nun's mouth.

"What do you think you're—" was all she had time to say before her voice was cut off.

Next Riley tied her hands to the back of the chair she was sitting in and drew the heavy curtains, while Jack took the papers on the table, a beautiful Bible bound in lambskin and a massively heavy treatise on the life of Saint Domingo of Guzmán and rolled them into a ball on the floor.

The nun watched the two soldiers with growing alarm.

"Whak g' you hink you're…" she mumbled under the gag.

When a substantial quantity of paper and wood had been piled in the middle of the room, Riley brought out his lighter. With a sharp twist he lit it in front of her face. "You didn't want to do it the nice way," he said calmly, "so we'll do it the nasty way. I'll burn this whole building down with you and your sisters in it. Then while the soldiers are on their way to put the fire out, my friend and I will take advantage of the confusion to rescue the prisoners. How does that sound to you?"

"*Gggggg!*"

"Oh, true… the gag." He turned to Jack. "Pity she didn't talk when she had the chance. Wouldn't you agree?"

"Well, I'm not really sure… I almost prefer it this way. One bloodsucker less in the world."

"Don't talk about her like that, Jack," Riley replied in a stage voice. "Let's be respectful, the poor thing is about to go and meet her maker."

"*GGGGGG!*"

He took a piece of paper, set it on fire with the lighter and dropped it on the pile. "See you in hell, Sister Divine Charity," he said in an icy voice, and walked toward the door. "And when you see your boss, tell him from me that he's doing a terrible job."

"*GGGGG! GGGGG!*"

He opened the door and went through calmly. Jack followed him and closed it behind him with a dull click.

In the studio the piled-up papers burned quickly, together with the leather bindings of the books, which began to give out a dense black smoke in preparation for bursting into flame.

The nun kept trying to scream under her gag.

The door opened again and Riley's face peered in to ask, "Did you say something?"

She was beginning to feel the heat from the emerging flames on her face.

"*GGGGGG!*"

Jack peered in after him. "I can't understand a word of what she's saying. Maybe it's the gag."

"What shall we do? Take it off?"

"*GGGGG!*"

"Whatever you say, Alex. You're the boss."

Riley feigned to think for a few seconds, which to the nun felt like an eternity.

"Okay," he said with an air of weariness. "Let's see what our friend has to say." He put his hands to the nape of the nun's neck and untied the gag.

"Yes! Yes!" She coughed. "I'll help you! I'll help you! But put that fire out!"

Riley moved to one side while Jack poured a jug of water he had found on the side table over the flames. He then stamped on the smoking embers. "Okay," he said as he untied her hands. "How can we get in and out of the church without being seen?"

The nun rubbed her eyes, which were irritated by the smoke. "You can't," she said.

"Here we go again!" said Jack bad-temperedly.

"It's the truth. The church of San Martín de Tours only has one entrance, the main one." She coughed again and added, "I swear." She crossed herself.

The two men exchanged a glance. She did not seem to be lying.

"Damn!" murmured Jack. He leaned on the closed window shutters. "We were so near…"

"There has to be a way," Alex said. "There always is."

"Well, you tell me. If there's only one entrance and it's under observation by soldiers, we'd need to be invisible."

"That would be nice." He grinned. "I'd love to be able to… to…"

"To what?" Jack asked after a few seconds, when Riley did not finish the sentence.

But Riley did not hear him. His gaze was fixed on the mother superior, who was wriggling in the chair, uncomfortable under the gaze of his amber eyes.

"What are you looking at?" she asked at last.

"What's up, Alex?"

Riley took a moment longer to stir from his reverie. Instead of answering, he asked the nun, "How many sisters are there in the convent?"

Sister Charity blinked in confusion. "What?"

"How many nuns are there here, in this convent?"

"Why… why do you ask?"

"How many?"

"Nineteen, not counting me."

Riley nodded distantly. With the ghost of a smile, he murmured, "Enough."

"Enough for what?" Jack asked.

His smile widened, forming wrinkles at the sides of his mouth. "To be invisible, my friend," he replied, and patted the other's shoulder. "To be invisible."

"You're crazy." Such was Jack's scathing reply when Riley had finished outlining his rescue plan. "There are a thousand things that could… no, that *will* go wrong."

"Tell me one."

"*Carallo.* To begin with, you're taking it for granted that the sentinels are blind idiots."

"It's the middle of the night, and I doubt they'll suspect a couple of nuns."

Jack opened his mouth again, but realized that Alex would counter any objection he made, however much he might be in the right. After all, he concluded, he could not think of a better plan himself.

"Okay…" he said resignedly. "What do we do?"

"The first thing is to wake up all the sisters, explain what we're going to do and get them to dress as fast as they can. You'll be in charge of that, Sister Charity."

The nun, now standing in front of the table, was composing her clothing and shaking off the flakes of ash that had fallen on her white habit. "No," she said without raising her head.

"Excuse me?"

"I said no," she repeated, and looked up at him.

Riley stepped forward to face her, his hazel eyes burning with fury.

"Don't mistake my courtesy for lack of determination, Sister Charity."

"I'll help you," she said, "if you help us."

"What?" Jack asked, thinking he could not have heard right.

"You want to get those friends of yours out of Belchite before the reds attack the village, don't you?"

Riley did not answer the rhetorical question. He was intrigued to hear what the nun was getting at.

"Well now," she went on, with her hands on her lap and looking at each of them in turn. "I'll help you, but in exchange I want you to help us too."

"Help you?" Jack asked suspiciously. "To do what?"
"To escape from Belchite. To cross the Republican Army lines and reach safety."

15

"You don't know what you're asking," said Riley.

"I've seen the soldiers of your army surrounding the village and I know we're completely besieged," the nun replied. "Unless there's a miracle," she added with a slight tremor in her voice, "Belchite will be destroyed."

"Not if the garrison surrenders first."

"You know perfectly well that isn't going to happen. That's why you're risking your lives to save your red friends in the church. Isn't that right?"

"They're not our friends," Jack corrected her," and neither are they *reds*, as far as we know. Quite honestly, we don't even know who they are."

She gave them a puzzled look."Then… why…?"

Jack shrugged."Does it matter?"

She half-closed her eyes, trying to gauge his sincerity.

"Do you understand how dangerous what you're asking might be, Sister Charity?" Alex put in. "If they catch us, they'll throw all of us in front of a firing squad."

"You and the others, no doubt about that. On the other hand, we can say you made us do it. After all," she added, clasping the little wooden cross that hung from her neck in a gesture of innocence that was almost comical, "we're just a handful of poor helpless sisters."

Riley shook his head. "Oh well…" he said resignedly, and looked at the sergeant. "Better be hung for a sheep as for a lamb, right? Anyway, we've got no alternative."

"But how the hell are we going to do it?" Jack burst out. "Getting into the church without being seen, freeing fifteen or twenty civilians and slipping out of the village without being found out is already all-but-impossible. To try doing it encumbered by a pack of old women dressed in white" – he gestured at the Mother Superior – "just guarantees we'll end up in front of a firing squad."

"I know Jack, I know… but we'll think of something. For the moment what we have to do is get into that church, and we need them for it."

"*We'll think of something?*" Jack repeated, frowning. "Are you serious?"

"Stop grumbling and let's be on our way. We have" – he consulted his watch, and his face took on a worried look – "less than five hours to do everything and get back to the camp before anybody finds out we're gone."

The nun left the studio, then went into the six shared dormitories one by one and ordered the sisters to get up, get dressed as fast as they could and head for the chapel as soon as possible.

Next the three of them went to this chapel, access to which was through an inner passage in the convent. It turned out to be bigger than expected, decorated with stained-glass windows and a series of paintings along the nave representing scenes of Christ's Passion.

As Riley sat down in the first row facing the altar, waiting for the nuns to arrive, he fleetingly thought that like many others across the length and breadth of the country, all those unique works of art would be destroyed in a matter of days, perhaps even hours. War did not only destroy living people but the memory of those who were already dead as well.

After a few minutes the first nuns appeared, a group of three who were whispering among themselves. They stopped short, their eyes like saucers, when they saw two men in black with blackened faces sitting beside the mother superior on the wooden benches and staring at them with almost identical surprise on their own faces.

"They're…they're…" stammered Jack.

"Novices," said Sister Charity. "This is a seminary for novices, and as you may realize it is not simply *a pack of old women dressed in white.*"

Although they were all dressed in the loose habits of the order, with only their faces showing under their wimples and veils   which in the case of the novices were also white   Jack was left speechless before the steady parade of young aspirant nuns. Many of them were beautiful, as well as victims of involuntary blushes as they passed in front of the two men, something which made them even more attractive in the eyes of the robust sergeant.

"I've died and gone to heaven…" he murmured without taking his eyes off them. "Now I understand why so many men want to become priests."

"Don't be crude," the nun scolded him with a frown.

"Pardon him," Riley said in his defense. "The poor man has spent months without... well, you know."

"Well, he can go without for another day," she retorted. "Because if he lays a finger on any of my girls..." She turned to Jack, making the sign of scissors with her fingers. "Do you understand me?"

"Sure... sure..." he answered, without taking his eyes of the girls, like a child staring at a jar of sweets.

The parade of novices ended after a few minutes with the appearance of three nuns. These were genuine nuns; according to Sister Charity as she introduced them to the two men. They were in charge of the education and guidance of the novices during their stay in the seminary.

When they were sure nobody was missing and all had taken their places on the chapel benches, the mother superior climbed up to the pulpit. After introducing Alex and Jack without going into too many details, she quickly explained what they were going to do that night, the reasons why and the consequences it would have for all of them.

The first reaction was of uneasy silence, followed by a growing confusion which ran like gunpowder amid whispers and expressions of disbelief. Very soon some began to look scandalized, while most seemed to believe they were still in bed, victims of a bad dream.

"Wait a moment!" Riley cut in, standing up and raising his hands to impose order. "I understand you'll have many doubts, but you'd better ask *us* whatever questions you have, not whoever's sitting beside you."

A nun as old and ill-favored as Sister Charity stood up aggressively and addressed the mother superior."Are you telling us we have to leave because a damned red says so?"

"No, Sister Grace," she said sharply. "Because I say so."

"But why?" She pointed at the two men. "Why are you paying any attention to them? They're the enemy! Don't you see?"

"Sister Grace, I see it perfectly well. If I'm doing this, it's for everyone's benefit, including yours."

"This has been my home for twenty years," she insisted. "Home for all of us, mother superior. We can't leave just like that and lose everything we've built up."

Riley decided to intervene. "I understand, sister. I understand this must be very hard for you... for all of you. But tomorrow, first thing in the morning, the Republican planes will come and start bombing the village, and then you won't be able to leave."

"But this is a convent!" she said. "Why would they bomb a convent?"

"They'll bomb everything," he explained with a heavy heart. "Houses, barracks, churches...there's no safe place in Belchite."

"The walls are strong," said another nun, who had been introduced as Sister Lucia. "Besides, we can take shelter in the cellars and wait for everything to pass. We have enough supplies and water."

Riley shook his head. "That doesn't matter. Even if the building withstood the bombing, which I doubt, tanks and twenty-five thousand Republican assault soldiers will attack after them, and then" – he scratched the back of his neck uncomfortably – "anything might happen."

"What do you mean?" asked a novice in one of the front rows. She looked barely eighteen.

He turned to the mother superior, begging her silently to throw him a line, but she seemed to be delighted that he was being forced to explain himself."Well... they..." He hesitated, searching for the right words. "Some are bad people who've been given guns and... well... you're all very... very..."

"Very...?"

"Very young and pretty. And they..." Alex swept his gaze along those innocent faces and was incapable of saying what he had to.

Impatiently, Sister Charity stepped forward. In a strong, clear voice she said, "Those red soldiers who're coming might kill us all... or even worse."

Sister Charity's forceful words had dispelled the doubts of the novices and the other nuns, and after a few complaints they went back to their rooms to gather together the few belongings they would be able to take with them.

Not ten minutes had passed when the last of them was standing at the front door listening to the final instructions the mother superior was giving, with the precision of a general rallying his troops.

Jack and Riley exchanged a glance of respect at this martial attitude of the nuns and novices. They would have liked to have seen it in their own men of the battalion.

"Don't worry," she was saying, offering a comforting gesture to each of them. "Trust in God and He will protect us. Do not be afraid."

The two soldiers took advantage of the moment to clean their hands and face in the basin beside the entrance.

An irate voice behind them said, "You don't respect anything, do you!"

Sister Grace was staring at them with arms akimbo and a deeply hostile expression on her face.

"We have to take off this shoe polish," Riley replied as he rubbed his hands. "You wouldn't have a bit of soap, would you?"

"But that's the basin of holy water!"

"You don't say!" cried Jack. He dipped his head into the water and out again. "Now I understand why I was burning!" he added with a shameless grin as the water dripped down his face.

The sister turned red with rage until she seemed about to explode."You're... you're—"

"Do you have what we asked for?"Riley cut her short brusquely.

The nun opened and shut her mouth several times like a fish out of water, searching for the right words to show her irritation, but this apparently was so great that she could find nothing in her monastic vocabulary that would not infringe some rule of the order. So she simply pointed to the pile of clothes she had left on one of the benches. Then she turned round and left to join the other Dominican nuns.

Jack finished wiping the last remnants of shoe polish off his face."Do you think I upset her?"he said.

"Who knows?" Riley shrugged. "These nuns are so grumpy, it's hard to know when they're really mad."

When they had finished cleaning up, the two friends took the clothes Sister Grace had brought them, put them on and presented themselves to the mother superior.

A fit of nervous giggling ran through the novices, and even Sister Charity had to press her lips so as not to do the same.

Before them, dressed in the habits of the order too short on one of them and too tight on the other – Alex and Jack looked like two particularly ugly bearded women who had taken holy orders after being expelled from some sleazy circus.

"Sister Riley and Sister Alcántara reporting for duty," Jack said and, as a final insult, he gave a salute in the military style.

"Holy Mother of God…" was the first thing the mother superior managed to say as she crossed herself. "May God pardon me for this offense."

Riley went up to the nun. "Can you help me with the wimple?" he asked. "My ears keep sticking out."

Jack ran his hand round his waist. "These clothes make me look fat," he said. "Don't you have any black ones?"

Sister Lucia put her hands to her head, shaking her head over and over. She pointed at him. "But what's going to happen?" she muttered. "You can see they're men from miles off! They even have beards!"

"That's true," agreed Sister Grace. "Besides" – she looked at Alex – "your boots show under the habit. And as for you," she added, this time to Jack, "well, you look as if you'd gone through the whole larder."

"We don't have time to go to the barber's," Riley said, "and these are the biggest habits you could find, right? We'll have to trust the darkness to protect us and that the watchmen will be paying more attention to the novices than to us."

"They'll notice," she insisted, shaking her head. "You stand out too much. We'll be caught, and then we'll all end up in front of the firing squad."

Riley gave a stoical shrug. "In that case," he said, putting his hand to the wooden crucifix which now hung round his neck, "I hope your boss will lend us a hand."

16

Bent over like ancient rheumatic women, concealed in the midst of that compact formation of nuns which resembled a phalanx, Riley and Jack walked with bowed heads, hiding beneath their nuns' habits and veils, hoping that the darkness and absence of lighting in the main street would prevent anybody becoming aware of their presence.

Slowly they covered the few dozen yards separating the plaza from Saint Martin of Tours, where the soldiers were on guard duty in front of the church.

The half-dozen legionnaires took up a defensive position as soon as the procession of nuns came into the plaza. Riley took a careful look to see what was going on and was able to see the disconcerted expression on the soldiers' faces. None of them had expected anything of the kind at that hour of the night.

"Stop there!" the sergeant of the squad called out. He raised his hand and strode to the head of the procession. "Who goes there?"

"What does it look like, young man?" the mother superior asked the legionnaire, who looked no more than twenty or twenty-one.

The answer caught the NCO by surprise; it seemed he was not used to being addressed by a nun in this way. He attempted vainly to sound authoritative. "Where are you going?" he demanded.

Sister Charity pointed at the building in front of them. "To the church," she replied in the same tone. "Where else do you think we'd be going?"

"You can't," the sergeant said, irritated by her condescending tone. "Don't you know there's a curfew? Nobody may leave their homes until six in the morning."

"As it happens, we aren't *nobody*." She turned with a wave toward the others. "And we have to go to the parish church for matins."

"At this hour?"

"Matins are celebrated very early in the morning, young man," she said, and went up closer to him with a confidential air. "And today is a very special day. Today we celebrate the day of Saint Bononio of Lucedio."

The sergeant did not appear very impressed. "I don't care if it's St Vitus' Day," he replied. "You can't be in the street during the curfew."

"Of course." Sister Charity nodded. "As soon as you stop questioning me we'll be able to go into the church, and then we won't be in the street."

"You can't go into the church. Go back to your convent and pray there."

The mother superior shook her head slowly from side to side. "I see you don't understand," she said. "The figure of Saint Bononio is in this church, not in the convent. That's why we have to pray there."

"Well, it's just not going to be possible, sister. I have orders that nobody is to go in there."

"I repeat, we aren't *nobody,*"she insisted, and went straight toward the church door with the aim of dodging the sergeant.

He reacted by seizing her arm."I told you, you can't go in."

"And I'm telling you that we must. Besides, yesterday Commander Trallero gave us permission to celebrate this mass."

This time the mention of the mayor and commander of the plaza had an immediate effect.

"The…commander?"

"That's right." The nun pointed down the street. "If you want, you can go and wake him up and ask him in person."

He hesitated for the first time.

"Oh, come on," Sister Charity urged him. "Go and ask him, we don't have all night. I'm sure he won't mind being woken up at three in the morning to know whether a few nuns are allowed to go and pray in the church."

The sergeant, obviously unsettled by the nun's domineering attitude, snorted in disgust."All right," he finally agreed, and moved aside. "Go on, then."

Without wasting a second, the mother superior made a sign to the other nuns and novices, and they set off toward the church.

When Riley and Jack passed the sergeant, he was still looking at the irritating nun and did not notice them one excessively tall and the other excessively stout – who would never have gone unnoticed in the daylight even if they had been hiding among the novices.

They were walking side by side, and after passing the legionnaire they exchanged a silent glance of relief. It seemed they had managed to deceive him, and only a few yards remained before they reached the church steps.

But at that moment the soldier's voice called out behind them, "Halt! Stop there!"

The young sergeant's order seemed to have been aimed straight at Riley's heart, since for a moment it ceased to beat.

Not daring to look up or turn around, but certain that they had been spotted, he put his hand into a fold of the habit and grasped the grip of the gun he carried in the waistband of his pants. "Get ready," he whispered to Jack. "You grab the sergeant and I'll go for the others. If we take them by surprise…"

"Shhh…wait," Jack whispered back.

Alex fell silent, in time to hear the legionnaire say to Sister Charity, "I can't let you go into the church alone." He whistled with two fingers and gestured to two of the sentinels to come quickly.

"But—" the nun began to protest.

The sergeant raised his hand, silencing her.

"Two of my men will accompany you during the mass," he said, and smiled maliciously. "The commander might have given you permission to pray at untimely hours, but nobody said you had to do it alone."

The two soldiers opened the church door, which was locked from the outside, and stayed on either side of the door while the nuns went in. Once they were all inside, the two legionnaires went in after them and closed the door anew with a heavy iron key more than a hand span long.

The inside of the church was completely dark, until the mother superior lit a few candles and a timid yellowish light began to spread throughout the nave. It revealed the rounded forms of the columns, the white marble altar, a great Christ on the cross hanging above it and the ordered wooden pews which took up practically all the space, separated by a central aisle. In spite of the dim light, Riley could make out a series of dark shapes lying in the aisle, which immediately began to rise and whisper among themselves.

"Here they are," Jack said in his ear.

Alex nodded in response. Taking great care to avoid being seen, he turned to confirm that the two legionnaires had stayed behind them and were standing by the door, some ten yards away.

Jack nodded in their direction. "We have to take care of those two," he hissed.

"We can't now," said Alex. "If we go near them, they'll see our faces."

Jack considered this for a few seconds, then said, "Well, let them come instead. You just follow my lead." All of a sudden, after a terrible imitation of a feminine swoon, he dropped to the floor and stayed there face down as though he had hit his head.

Riley's eyes opened wide. For a moment he tried to hold his friend up, not having a clear idea about what he intended to do, until he saw the novices forming a circle around him.

"Call the soldiers," Riley told the one nearest to him. "Tell them to come and help."

She looked at him in confusion, not really knowing what he meant, so that Alex had to repeat it, this time with a wink which made the novice blush.

"Help!" she cried. Then, raising her hand, "Gentlemen, help us get our sister to her feet, please, she's fainted."

The two soldiers looked at one another, perplexed. But they were young too, and a girl calling for help is always a girl calling for help, even when she is wearing a nun's habit. It did not take them as much as two seconds to decide; they slung their rifles over their shoulders and made their way through the circle of novices.

"Jesus, what a whale!" said one of them in astonishment.

"It'd take a truck to move her," the other agreed.

Then the first one bent and with some effort tugged at her arm to turn her over. "Do you feel all right, sister?" he asked.

His astonishment was overwhelming when he turned her on her back and came face to face with Jack's chubby, bearded features, twisted into a frown.

"Who did you call a whale?"

The legionnaire jumped as if he had found a snake under a rock, and at the moment his hand moved toward his rifle Jack brought out his Tokarev pistol and pressed it against his chest with the speed of lightning.

The second soldier took a moment too long before he reacted, and only did it when he saw the gun in the hands of the supposed nun. He too reached instinctively for his rifle and took a step back, but in his case it was the cold touch of steel at the back of his neck that made him desist. That, and Riley's voice behind him. "As my fellow countrymen say," he warned, cocking his Colt, "I wouldn't do it if I were you, stranger."

17

"Right. So now what?"That was the question on everyone's minds, and the fact that it was Sister Charity who posed it was mere chance.

While the novices and nuns took care of the civilians, checking that they were all well and reassuring them, Riley, Jack and the mother superior joined Eustaquio, who had assumed leadership of the family group, on one side of the nave. They had explained to him as soon as they had seen him that they had sent his son Javier to the Lincoln camp with a personal message for Captain Shaw. This explained what had happened and asked him to take care of the boy while they were on their way back.

"Will he be all right?" Eustaquio had asked them, anxiously twisting his beret in his hands.

"Better than we are," Jack had assured him, patting his shoulder. "Captain Shaw is a great guy. Your son will be perfectly okay."

The villager still could not believe that the two men had risked their lives to rescue him and his family simply because they had given their word the night before. He had thanked them so many times and in so many different ways that Riley had to threaten him to make him stop.

Inside the church, apart from the nine adults, there were six children aged between four and twelve, who were mostly asleep like little angels. Although luckily there was no baby there who might cry at the worst possible moment, these children represented a complication they would rather have avoided.

"Now we'll get out of here," Riley replied to the nun's question.

"Yes, but how?"

"Through the door, naturally."

Sister Charity folded her arms. "Are you trying to be funny?"

"Not at all. It's just that there's nothing else we can do. We can't stay here, and we've already checked that there's no other way out and the windows are barred, so the only way we can leave is by the main door."

"But how?" Eustaquio insisted.

"We're still working on it." He pointed at Jack. "But don't worry, we'll find a way."

Jack turned to him, eyebrows raised. "Oh, yeah?"

"Of course," Alex said. He leant against a column. "Actually, all we have to do is divide up the problem. First we decide what we want to do, then we identify the elements we can count on, and finally we choose how to use those elements to overcome the obstacles."

"I'm lost already."

"Me too," said Eustaquio.

"Let's see," Sister Charity said instead. She frowned, looking interested. "You mean, first we have to decide what we want. Well, that's easy. We want to leave the church, then

Belchite, then cross the red lines and finally get to Zaragoza. Am I leaving anything out?"

"And do it without being seen," Jack reminded her. "But yes, I'd say that's about it."

"Very well," said Riley. "Now we have to work out what we could use to manage it."

"We have our guns, and the Mausers we got from those two," said Jack. He nodded in the direction of the soldiers, who were gagged and tied up to one of the columns.

Riley raised his right thumb. "What else?"

"Legionnaires' clothes," Eustaquio added.

Riley raised another finger.

"Nineteen nun's habits," Jack put in, and earned himself a look of censure from the mother superior.

"And there might be one or two robes belonging to the parish priest in the vestry, right?" said Eustaquio.

"Well, with all this we could fit out a whole procession," suggested Jack, half in jest, half in earnest. "That would put them off for sure."

"I don't know whether it would be very discreet," said Riley.

"And the truck?" the nun asked. "I've seen one parked on the other side of the plaza. With that we could reach Zaragoza in a jiffy."

"That's true," Jack admitted reluctantly. "But the problem would be making the best part of forty people get on it without the sentinels raising the alarm, then manage to leave the village without being shot, and then cross the Republican lines without them shooting us again thinking we're the enemy."

"Well, now…" muttered Riley thoughtfully. He scratched his beard. "I don't have an answer yet for items two and three, but I think I know how we can manage the first."

"Are you serious?"

"Totally. When it comes to it, there's only one sergeant and four soldiers between us and the trucks."

"Are you proposing we get out of here shooting?" Sister Charity was shocked.

"Not exactly."

"Then how, exactly?" Eustaquio wanted to know.

Riley glanced at Sister Charity with the hint of a smile.

18

Less than an hour after the church door had closed it opened again. Out of it, two by two, walking with short silent steps and heads bowed, came the twenty-odd nuns.

But instead of heading for the convent they had started from, they paraded with Sisters Charity, Grace and Lucía at their head directly toward where the four legionnaires and the sergeant were keeping watch in the center of the plaza.

"Finished your prayers, then, sister?" the NCO said to the mother superior.

"That's right. Although today is a very special day for us, and we would like to share it with you." She looked aside to include the curious soldiers, who had come closer to listen to the conversation.

The sergeant looked at her in surprise. "Share? Share what?"

"The canticles to Saint Bononio, of course," she said as if stating the obvious. "The novice sisters have been very insistent that they would like to sing a canticle to these handsome soldiers."

"They said that?" The sergeant's gaze strayed from the mother superior's eyes, and perhaps in contrast to the plain nun, it seemed to him that behind her there was assembled a choir of virginal cherubs framed in white veils."It's not possible…" He hesitated, looking from the nun to the young novices who were looking back at him in turn. "The curfew…"

"Let them, sergeant," one of the soldiers asked behind him. He rearranged his cap more becomingly. "Let the girls sing."

"Yeah," said another. "Let'em sing, sarge, don't be a wet blanket."

He spun around. "Silence!"

"Please…" one of the novices pleaded in her sweet voice, as if it were something really important to her. "Just one song."

"Sarge… for the sake of your dead," the soldier insisted with his hand on his heart. "Let'em sing a little song…"

The sergeant clicked his tongue in annoyance, then gave in at last. "All right." Raising his finger, he added, "Just one, then you go back to your convent and leave us alone once and for all. Understood?"

Sister Charity gave an exaggerated smile, as if this were wonderful news. Then she turned and finished arranging the novices into a wide semicircle around the legionnaires, who were dusting down their clothes and tucking in their shirts, overwhelmed by this array of beauty.

When they were all standing where the mother superior wanted them to, at her command they began to sing the first verses of a hymn, to the rhythm of an imaginary baton:

Christ the Lord is love indeed
Humble charity, sweet to learn
Before the eyes of God himself
He gave the poor his gift

Following Jesus's good works
Given to the poor along his way
A life to live, a tale to tell
In the service of love itself

Walking along the path of Faith
From the trust in God himself
Trinity dwelling within his heart
A life that's lived in love of God

A mark which will fore'er endure
Molded by dear love itself
In answer to the call they heard
His work of love spread wider far

When the novices had finished chanting the last verse of the hymn, none of the soldiers was given the chance to applaud. Taking advantage of the distraction and the fact that the choir had placed itself so as to hide the entrance to the church, Riley and Jack took the sentinels from behind. They had trustingly left their guns to one side while enjoying the performance. They had no chance to resist, and even when they were firmly tied up and gagged by Eustaquio and his nephew — one Adalberto, who looked less than eighteen — they could not understand what was going on and what relation the angelic novices could have with those two guys dressed in black who seemed to be in command of the whole business.

"Go and fetch everybody," Riley said to Eustaquio. "And make sure they do it in silence. Not a word."

"What about those two?" he asked, referring to the two soldiers who were still tied up inside the church. "What do we do with them?"

"Nothing. Just make sure they're still well gagged."

The farmer nodded and nudged Adalberto, who was busy emptying the soldiers' pockets and had already helped himself to a packet of tobacco, some matches, a box of licorice lozenges and a jackknife with a mother-of-pearl handle.

"Leave that and come with me," he urged. "You'll have plenty of time for stealing when you're older."

"We ought to kill them," said the young man. He was looking admiringly at the blade of the knife he had taken from one of the legionnaires. "Nobody would know."

"We're not going to kill anybody here," Alex said firmly. "Least of all someone helpless."

"Helpless?" he asked in disbelief. "They'd shoot us all without blinking an eye if they were ordered to."

"I know. But even so, we're not going to execute them in cold blood."

"They'd have done it," the young man insisted. He held the knife close to the sergeant's neck, with a homicidal glint in his eye.

"I said no, and that's that," Alex repeated, and in a brusque movement took the knife from Adalberto. "Now go and help your uncle bring everybody."

Grudgingly, the young man put the knife back in his pocket and ran after his uncle, who was already halfway back to the church. When Riley turned, he saw Sister Charity staring at him as if she had just seen him for the first time.

"What is it?" he asked.

The nun did not reply. Instead she asked, "What about us? What do we do now?"

Riley pointed to the other side of the plaza."Get on the truck. Jack will go with you."

She looked thoughtfully at the T69 Hispano-Suiza, whose back was covered by canvas."We'll be pretty tightly-packed," she said, assessing the size of the vehicle. "There are nearly forty of us."

"We'll all fit in, don't worry," Alex assured her. "Now you go with Jack. We have no time to lose."

"Follow me," Jack beckoned the nuns.

Riley waited for a moment, watching Jack leading the nuns after him like a chubby Pied Piper of Hamelin. When they were some way ahead, he crouched down in front of the sergeant, who was glaring at him from the floor with indescribable hatred."You, come with me," he said. He grabbed his arm and forced him to stand, then went a few yards away, almost dragging him with him. Pushing him roughly, he forced him to sit down on the cobbles and brought out the rough map of Belchite which Eustaquio's son had drawn for him a few hours before."I'm going to ask you some questions about the situation of your troops in the village," he said as he took off the gag, "and I want you to answer me quickly and without hesitation. If you don't, "he added as he took out a hunting knife from its sheath at his belt, "I'll hurt you. Is that clear?"

"I'm not going to tell you anything, you fucking red," the legionnaire barked.

Riley put the knife to the soldier's crotch. "You don't believe me?" he said, pressing the steel tip against his testicles as he spoke. "What I told that boy is only partly true, don't misunderstand me. To begin with, I'm not going to kill you, but if I press just a little more I can cut your balls off. How's that? A neutered soldier. You'd end up as the whore for the rest of the troop."

The sergeant struggled uselessly, trying to free himself from his bonds and get the knife away from his private parts. "You're a son of a bitch," he muttered under his breath.

"Oh, I know that," Riley admitted. "But just for now I'm the one with the knife in his hand and his balls where they ought to be, unlike yours in a moment."

The legionnaire looked fleetingly in the direction of the other soldiers, immobilized inside the wall of sandbags and out of his sight.

"If you don't talk, they will," Alex said, "and you'll have lost your manhood for nothing."

"I'm not going to tell you jack shit," the sergeant repeated. "Fucking re—"

Before he could finish, Riley took out his gun. Holding it by the barrel, he gave him a blow on the head with the butt which knocked him unconscious straight away. Then he made a cut on the sergeant's palm which started bleeding at once, and rubbed the knife in it until it was covered in blood. "It had to be the hard way, didn't it?" he said in a low voice, shaking his head as he worked.

Once he had finished he gagged the legionnaire again, got to his feet and walked over to the other four soldiers, who might not have seen what had happened but had heard quite clearly what had been said. He went to stand in front of the first of them. "I'm going to ask you a few questions about the situation of your troops in the village," he said, using the same words he had used with the sergeant, with the map in one hand and the knife in the other and deliberately letting the blood trickle down the blade and drip on the floor. "And I want you to answer quickly and without—"He did not need to end the sentence for the soldier to begin pointing things out on the map.

Eustaquio and his extensive family left the church, crossed the plaza at a run and got into the back of the truck. Here they shared the space with the nuns. At the same time Riley led the four soldiers into the church, having also made them carry the body of the unconscious sergeant.

"Is everybody here?" he asked Jack when he came back carrying a couple of legionnaire's shirts.

He stared at Riley's bloodied right hand. "I think so, but… what have you done to the guards?"

"Locked them up in the vestry. Here." He handed him one of the khaki shirts. "Put this on. It's not your size, but it'll pass in the dark."

Jack took it, but he was still looking at Riley's hand. "And the blood? Did you…?"

"I'll tell you later." He opened the door with a creak and climbed up behind the wheel. "Now climb in and let's get out of here as fast as we can, before another patrol appears and rains on our parade."

Jack got in beside him. "Okay, but what's the plan?"

"There's no plan."

"There's no plan?" he asked in bewilderment.

"Not exactly," Alex corrected himself. "The only plan is to get out of here."

"So…" He pointed toward the street which led away from the plaza to the north.

Riley nodded. "Let's go slowly while we can. That way they'll think we're one of them."

"And if we're spotted?"

"In that case, step on it and pray that they don't block the street."

"Step on it and pray…" Jack repeated with a humorless smile. "How is it that you're a lieutenant and I'm a sergeant?"

"Because I'm taller."

19

Riley asked Eustaquio to go with them in the cab. Sitting between him and Jack, he told them the shortest way out of the village while the engine finished warming up. "Straight on this way" – he pointed ahead – "to San Salvador Plaza. Then under the San Roque Arch, then out on to the road to Codo."

Alex nodded, engaged first gear and gently pressed the accelerator until the hundred and fifty horsepower of the Hispano-Suiza propelled the wheels over the cobblestones, moving on slowly in the direction Eustaquio had indicated.

From the moment he started the engine, there was no way back. Someone was sure to hear the gravelly purr and wonder where the truck was going in the middle of the night. If they were not outside the village in a couple of minutes, they would never get out.

Rattling on the cobbles, they reached Santa Ana Street, which was so narrow that the truck's roof passed only inches below the lowest balconies.

"It's pretty close," said Jack hanging out of the window.

"Well, it gets even narrower further on," Eustaquio pointed out. "At the San Roque arch."

Alex turned to him. "Why didn't you tell me before?" he said reproachfully. "We could have taken a different route."

The farmer shook his head. "They're all the same, *maestro*. Except the Main Street, but there are barricades up there."

"Great..." he said, and leant out of the window when he heard the canvas covering the cargo compartment full of fugitives scrape a lamppost on the wall.

At not much more than walking pace, the truck threaded the narrow street and finally came out into San Salvador Plaza. And there once again, exactly where they had seen them earlier that same night, were the two Moorish sentinels with their unmistakable red caps. On this occasion they were looking in the direction of the alley where the truck was emerging, rattling over the uneven pavement.

"Moors..." Jack muttered in warning. He was unable to hide the scorn in his voice.

"I can see them..." Riley said without slowing down. "Don't do or say anything. Don't even look at them."

Jack nodded and clenched his jaw, and Eustaquio huddled down into his seat.

The two sentinels stood up when they saw that the approaching truck did not have the slightest intention of stopping. One of them, who wore a corporal's stripes, took a step forward, but did not place himself directly in front of the truck. He looked toward the cabin and raised his right hand to stop them.

"Oh my god..." muttered Eustaquio.

Riley ignored the soldier's order. Without lifting his foot off the accelerator, he carried on in a straight line. When he drew alongside the two Moorish guards, he simply put his hand out of the window and smiled broadly as if they were old comrades in arms.

"Stop there!" the corporal shouted when he realized they were not stopping. "Password!"

Once again Riley put his hand out of the window, but this time to show them his watch and give it a couple of pats with his finger. *I'm late*, the gesture said.

Of course he did not know the password they wanted, and in addition he did not dare to speak in case these two noticed his American accent, so he simply mimed and kept going.

"Stop!" the corporal shouted again as Riley's truck passed beside him. "Stop or I shoot!"

In the rearview mirror Alex saw the two soldiers raising their rifles to their shoulders and aiming in their direction.

"Shit," he muttered under his breath, and stepped hard on the brakes. This caused a small tumult at the rear of the truck which did not pass unnoticed by the guards.

"Get off the truck!" the corporal ordered. He was gaunt and skinny, with several days' growth of beard and distrustful eyes. "Put your hands up!"

The two sentinels positioned themselves beside the door, aiming their Mausers at the men in the cab.

Riley leaned on the window as if he were arguing with a traffic policeman. "Come on, man, can't you see I'm in a hurry? The general has ordered me to transport some prisoners and—"

"Password!" the other interrupted him.

"I've forgotten," he admitted, putting on his best innocent smile.

"Get off the truck!" the Moor repeated, raising his voice still more. "Now!"

"Okay, pal," he said and gestured to the guard to calm down. "I'm coming…"

At that precise moment, a child's sob at the rear of the truck caught the attention of the two soldiers. They turned immediately.

Riley needed no more. That brief instant of confusion was enough to let him pull his gun out and point it at the two soldiers from the window."Put your guns down!" he shouted.

Far from obeying, they turned their rifles on him and opened fire, all the time cursing in Arabic.

The windshield shattered into a thousand pieces.

Riley's reflexes were prompt enough to make him crouch down behind the door, but even so, one of the bullets went through the panel and hit him in the right thigh, tearing off cloth and flesh.

Then two pistol shots sounded a few yards away, and Riley knew that Jack was firing in response.

Without thinking twice, he flung the door open. Before he had taken aim, he was already firing his Colt in the direction of the soldiers. Sensing rather than seeing the two white silhouettes of the Moors amid the cloud of gun smoke, he emptied the magazine, shooting until the hammer clicked on an empty chamber.

The shootout could have lasted no more than ten seconds, but the blast of the guns in that limited space still boomed in his ears. But what was more serious, he thought as the smoke disappeared and he looked without a trace of remorse at the two broken bodies of the soldiers on the cobblestones, was that the shots had woken up every last man, woman and child in Belchite. Their chances of getting out of the village alive, already slim enough, had just been dramatically reduced.

Jack hurried to him. "Are you all right?" he called. His voice seemed to be coming from miles away.

Riley looked up and saw his friend standing at the foot of the cabin with the Tokarev still smoking in his hand.

He touched his thigh. "More or less. I've been hit in the leg, but it doesn't look serious."

"Can you drive?"

"I think so." He took out a handkerchief from his pocket and proceeded to tie it around the wound.

"Well then, let's get out of here right away," Jack urged him climbing back into the truck. "This is going to get ugly before too long."

Riley did not even bother to reply. He slammed the door shut, put the truck into first gear and stepped on the accelerator. Beside him Eustaquio seemed to be in a state of shock, hunched in his seat, but Riley had no time to worry about him. "Get rid of the glass!" he ordered instead as the truck started to move lazily toward the way out of the plaza.

"What?"

"The glass!" He pointed at the broken windshield. "Get rid of the bits that are left!"

Eustaquio needed a moment to come out of his stupor and understand what Riley meant.

What had been the windshield was now a pile of sharp glass shards, hanging precariously from their rubber frame. If they were not removed, the rattling of the truck's progress would end up dislodging those shards on top of them.

"Stop! Stop!" someone cried from somewhere to his left. Immediately he heard the unmistakable sound of a Mauser firing, like a giant's dull handclap.

"Get down!" ordered Jack. He turned to face the back of the truck. "Everybody get down!"

Riley kept all his attention on the wheel and on the narrow street that led out of the village. The street was more like an alleyway, even narrower than the one they had come by. But that was not the worst thing.

As the man huddled beside him in the seat with his face slack-jawed had anticipated, the end of the street was marked by an arch which joined both sides. Centuries ago it must have been one of the gates of the walled village.

"Stop!" Eustaquio yelled. "We won't get through!"

Jack, on the other hand, shouted, "Faster!"

Riley moved into third gear. Pressing the pedal to its limit, he headed toward the arch.

As their speed increased there was no way of driving carefully, so now the sides of the truck bumped into the walls, knocking off lamps, latticed windows, or anything that stood out a few inches from the wall. The narrow arch was approaching fast, and it looked narrower every moment.

"Faster!" Jack shouted again above the deafening noise.

"I'm going as fast as I can!"

New shots sounded behind them, and someone cried out in pain at the back of the truck.

"They hit someone!" cried Eustaquio in alarm. He turned in his seat. "They hit someone!"

"We can't do anything now!" Jack said.

A group of soldiers appeared on the other side of the arch they still had to go through, and moving into the middle of the street they pointed their rifles at the truck.

"Switch on the headlights!" yelled Jack.

But before he had finished saying it, Riley's hand was already searching for the switch on the dashboard, and a second later the powerful headlights of the Hispano-Suiza illuminated the soldiers, giving them an almost ghostly appearance.

The National soldiers opened fire in unison, but dazzled by the truck's headlights, they aimed at the vehicle's body, and the bullets hit the radiator, the bumper and the roof like a brief, violent hailstorm.

Jack fired back on them with his Tokarev T-33. He did not hit anything but at least made them get out of the way.

At that moment they reached the arch, and the metal fenders of the front wheels screeched against the walls which hemmed them in, disintegrating and at the same time leaving a whitish groove on the stone.

"Hold on!" Alex shouted in warning.

Jack wondered about the reason behind the warning when the answer materialized in the form of a brutal impact which shook the whole truck. From the back came an outbreak of bumps and moans.

"Maria!" cried Eustaquio, staring back from his seat. "You all right?"

The roof of the cargo compartment had crashed into the lower part of the arch, and although the steel bars which held up the canvas roof had bent backward, the truck had stuck in a space too small for its size, and was now struggling to emerge in the way a wounded animal might try to escape from a trap.

A new burst of rifle fire came from the rearguard, and the cries of panic from nuns and civilians rose above the roaring of the engine, which sounded as if it were about to explode.

"Go faster, *carallo*!" Jack yelled at him. "Faster!"

Riley was already stepping on the accelerator with all his might. The vehicle had not completely stopped, but was dragging itself on, screeching and complaining with the terrible effort it was being forced to make.

Alex's muscles tensed like steel cables, perspiration ran down his forehead, and his eyes were fixed on the darkness of the field which spread beyond that damned stone arch they were stuck in. His whole being was focused on getting the truck through that last obstacle, but the more it moved on, the slower it went, and in spite of all that effort they seemed doomed to remain trapped in that accursed arch.

Finally the truck stopped, and although Riley went on stepping on the accelerator the vehicle refused to move a single inch further forward.

Then from the outer corners of the arch and just a few yards ahead of them, a scattering of legionnaires appeared aiming their guns and firing at close range at the cab.

The three occupants threw themselves to the floor as soon as they saw their attackers, and a fresh shower of glass fell on the fugitives.

They were trapped.

20

"Oh my God..." stammered Eustaquio, huddled in a ball on the floor of the cabin. "My God, my God..."

A new salvo of shots burst against the cabin, but this time the legionnaires had aimed at the truck's headlights. They would not be able to dazzle them a second time.

Riley and Jack took advantage of that moment of cover to reload their guns with a second magazine.

"They're going to wipe us out!" cried Jack.

Riley cocked his Colt. Breathing heavily, he shouted to his friend, "Cover me!"

"What? You're not gonna—"

"I said *cover me*!" he roared.

Jack did as he was told, poked his head out and started shooting at the soldiers. He hit one, who fell back, and forced the others to seek shelter round the corner.

Taking advantage of the moment, Riley stood up in the cabin, jumped on the hood of the truck and from there down to the cobbled street. He landed on his wounded leg and muffled a cry of pain. But he did not stop, and while Jack went on firing behind him, he rounded the corner where the legionnaires were hiding. Surprised at the unexpected appearance of the American, they had no time to react when he pointed his gun at them and felled them with two point-blank shots.

Then a new fusillade crashed against the rear of the truck. Alex put his gun away, grabbed a rifle from one of the fallen men and threw himself to the ground. The only free space was beneath the truck, so he crept under the front and was able to make out dozens of shadows hurrying toward them down the narrow street. He drew back the bolt of the Mauser to put a bullet in the chamber, aimed at the closest figure, and fired.

One of the soldiers gave a scream of pain and fell.

When they saw this, all those behind him sought cover as best they could inside doors and behind balustrades. Alex was still able to fire two more shots before they discovered him under the truck and opened fire on him.

A rain of bullets fell on the lower body of the truck, slicing off shards of stone as they hit the pavement. One of these bullets ended up in the offside rear tire so that it burst, causing that part of the truck to subside several inches toward the ground.

Riley was taken aback, surprised by this unexpected effect, until his mind succeeded in making sense of it. Then he crawled back until he could get to his feet again and went to stand in front of the vehicle so that his friend could see him. "Jack, get behind the wheel and hit the gas!" he shouted.

"But we're stuck!"

"I know! Just do what I say!"

And although he did not understand why, Jack obediently slid to the other side of the cabin and brought the engine to roaring life once again.

Alex threw himself under the vehicle a second time. But this time he ignored the soldiers firing at him and instead aimed at the other tire and opened fire.

Immediately the rear of the truck sank far enough to disengage the roof from the top of the arch, and the truck shot forward like a champagne cork flying free after the bottle has been shaken hard.

The underside of the Hispano-Suiza brushed over Riley's head where he was still lying in the middle of the road.

Then, more than fifty yards along the road out of the village, the truck stopped with a screech of brakes and Jack's head emerged from the driver's window. "Alex, come on, *carallo*!" he shouted, waving his arms. "What are you waiting for!"

He did not have to ask twice. Alex crawled back to the corner, fired the last two bullets left in the magazine, dropped the rifle, and ran as though pursued by the devil until he reached the rear of the truck and heaved himself into it.

A second later the vehicle was bouncing forward along the dirt road to Codo, heading deeper into the darkness and away from the village of Belchite, from which sporadic shots were still being fired, although their attackers seemed to be undecided as to whether to chase them into the night.

Inside the cargo compartment, where the nuns and Eustaquio's family were huddled, there was barely room to move. Darkness was complete, covered as they were by that torn and perforated canvas, and there were moans of pain and fear. The truck, rolling on its rims without any rear tires to act as cushions, was shaking like a wild horse trying to free itself of its rider, and paradoxically, the fact that they were so crowded together prevented anyone from falling out.

For a moment Riley had the terrible thought that this crazy escape had turned out to be a disaster, and that all those good people crowding around him would have fared better staying in Belchite."Is anyone hurt?" he asked toward the darkness uneasily, guessing what the answer might be.

Several moans were the immediate reply, followed by a funereal silence that sounded ominous.

"Mister Riley?" said a familiar voice. "Is that you?"

"Sister Charity?" he answered, and was surprised at how glad he was to hear her voice.

"Yes, it's me," she said. "What happened? Are we out of Belchite yet?"

Riley nodded in the dark, pointlessly."Yes, we're outside it now."

"Oh, God bless us!" she cried. "Sisters! We're out of the village!" she repeated more loudly.

In response a chorus of hallelujahs and blessings ran from mouth to mouth. "Blessed be our Lord Jesus Christ who has protected us!"

"Yeah, sure, Jesus Christ…" murmured Riley. "Are you okay? Is anybody hurt?"

"I don't know."

"Well, find out!" Alex ordered.

"And you?" the nun asked him. To his surprise there was sincere concern in her voice. "You aren't wounded?"

"I got hit in the leg, but I'm fine. It's just a scratch."

"Let me take a look," she said, and took his arm.

"Later, later," he said rather uncomfortably. "Take care of the others first."As he said this, he realized with some puzzlement that the truck's speed was progressively decreasing. A few seconds later, with a mechanical groan, it stopped altogether."What the hell…?" he muttered. He lifted the canvas and saw that the village was not much more than half a mile away. Still too close.

Taking care not to put his weight on his injured leg, he jumped down and went to the cab. When he reached it, Eustaquio asked him how his wife and daughters were, and when Alex did not know what to say to him, he jumped out of his seat and ran to the rear.

Meanwhile Jack was bent down under the hood examining the entrails of the huge engine. From it a cloud of white smoke was rising.

"What's up?" Riley asked. "Why have we stopped?"

"That's what I'd like to know myself," his friend replied. "Can you give me some light?"

Riley climbed on the bumper, lit his lighter and held it close to the engine, which smelt strongly of burning oil.

Cautiously Jack put his hand in and tested wires, tubes and fitments, checking there was nothing loose.

"Do you know anything about engines?" Riley asked after watching him fiddle around for a while.

"Not a thing," Jack admitted. He looked up. "What about you?"

Even with their deficiencies in the field of automobile mechanics, it did not take them long to realize that a bullet must have pierced some key part of the cooling system and the engine had overheated until it could go no longer. As a result they were forced to make everybody get off the truck and go on in the direction of the Republican lines.

In the process they were able to establish that the list of injured, luckily, was considerably shorter than they had feared. The rear door of the truck was bullet-proofed with a thick steel panel, which had acted as a parapet and saved the occupants from the National bullets. Most of the wounds were from the sharp fragments which had flown everywhere, and the few bruises were simply the result of the truck's bumpy progress.

However, the aged Sister Lucía had been unlucky enough to have several people fall on top of her at some point during the escape and had apparently fractured a hip. Prostrate on the ground beside the truck, she was bemoaning her misfortune with a circle of novices and nuns around her tending to her and trying to comfort her."Aaah…Oh my God, aaah…" she sobbed in pain.

"Easy, sister," Sister Charity said as she stroked her forehead. "You'll get better, don't worry."

"Confession…" she muttered, clutching the cross that hung from her neck. "Confession…"

"Don't exaggerate, Sister Lucía. You're not going to die." The mother superior gave her a reassuring smile. Turning to Riley she said, "We have to take her to a doctor."

The Lieutenant of the Lincoln Brigade turned to look at the Republican positions, then at Belchite. He calculated they must be midway between the two. The village was still too close for comfort, and if some rebel officer came out in pursuit of them searching for revenge, even on foot it would take him just a few minutes to catch up with them. "We have to leave right now," he said. "So we'll have to carry her."

"With a broken hip and at her age," Sister Charity argued, "you can't think of carrying her like a sack of potatoes. She'd die of pain."

"Well, you'll have to excuse me, sister, but we forgot to bring a wheelchair."

She frowned at his tone. "Don't you get sarcastic with me, young man, and try to be useful instead of funny."

Riley raised his finger, ready with an angry reply, but at that moment someone shut the rear door of the truck with a loud thud and he thought of a way they could carry the injured nun. "Maybe if…" he muttered. He left the nun's side and climbed into the cargo compartment. "Jack, lend me a hand with this." He pulled out his knife and tore off a large piece of canvas. "Find some sticks," he added to Eustaquio and some of his relatives, who were staring at the scene from a distance. "We're going to make a stretcher."

Once the stretcher was made they put Sister Lucía on it. With four of the men carrying it they set out, with the two men leading them, leaving the truck and heading on foot toward the Republican lines.

Jack indicated the slowly brightening sky to the east. "It's getting lighter."

"I can see that."

Jack looked back, toward that ill-assorted column of refugees walking in silence in the twilight, made up of women, children, a few men and about twenty nuns who in their white clothing looked like banshees traveling through the night."We're going very slowly," he noted uneasily. "Dawn's going to catch us on the way."

"Hmm."

"We're not going to get back in time, Alex. Marty will find out, the general will find out, and you and I will find ourselves in front of a court martial."

Riley nodded. Jack opened his mouth ready to say something more, but ended up saving his breath."Hmm," he said instead, with the same air of fatality.

At that moment Eustaquio came up to them from behind, carrying one of his daughters on his shoulders."I…" – he cleared his throat in embarrassment – "I'm really grateful… to both of you, for getting us out of the village."

"You're welcome, pal," Riley said. "We got you into this mess. We're just trying to fix it and do the right thing."

The peasant snorted."The right thing…" he repeated, as if it were the name of a mythical city. "Here nobody does the right thing. Not even them." He waved toward the nuns. "They wouldn't have cared one way or the other if we'd all been shot, since we're just reds to them. Deep down, they're just like the fascists."

Jack looked at him before asking, "And suppose they'd been raped and murdered by the anarchists… would you have done anything to help them?"

Eustaquio gave him a look heavy with guilt, then bowed his head."Is it very far?" he asked, when the echo of the reproach had faded in his ears.

"Hard to say," Riley replied. "There isn't a painted line on the ground marking the front."

"How will we know we've crossed it?"

"Well, we'd have to…" He left the sentence unfinished, because a group of shadows rose from the underbrush on both sides of the path just a few yards ahead of them.

"Stop right there!" someone ordered. "Who goes there?"

Riley stopped at once. "Soldiers of the Republic! From the Lincoln Battalion!"

"Password!" the same voice demanded in a strong German accent.

"Paprika!" Jack said in reply.

For a few endless seconds the sentinel seemed to ponder the answer, and when they were beginning to fear that they would be told it was not the up-to-date password, he said, "Hot!"

The two men breathed out heavily in relief, and the swaying light of a lantern advanced toward them in the soldier's hands. When he was close he shone the light directly on them.

They had not expected what followed.

The sentinel shouted at the top of his voice, "It's a trap! They're legionnaires!"

Alex and Jack felt the impulse to turn in search of the legionnaires the sentinel was talking about. It took a second more before they realized he was talking about them. Unforgivably, they had overlooked the fact that they were still wearing the shirts belonging to the soldiers they had left tied up in the village.

Riley opened his mouth to try to clear up the misunderstanding, but before he could say a word, someone fired.

21

"Hold your fire!" Riley shouted above the chorus of yelling that had broken out behind him. "We're your own people, goddammit! Hold your fire!"

"We've got civilians with us!" shouted Jack beside him. "Women and children! Don't shoot, *cagondiez*!"

"Identify yourselves!" a voice barked out behind the lantern.

"Lieutenant Riley and Sergeant Alcántara of the Lincoln Battalion!" cried Alex. "We were on patrol!"

The sentinel seemed to consider this reply, going over the names to see if they sounded familiar. "And what about all those people?" he asked, still distrustfully. "Where are they from?"

"They're refugees from Belchite."

The light came a few yards closer, illuminating the group. "B...but half of them are nuns!" he said incredulously.

"They're refugees and they're in my charge," Alex said. Feeling more confident, he asked, "And who are you, soldier?"

"Corporal Stern. Thaelmann Brigade."

"German?"

"Austrian."

Riley went up to him and stood in front of him with his hands behind his back. The corporal was a young man with a red badge on his lapel, a Lenin-style goatee and the round glasses of an intellectual. The archetypal Communist Party member."Very well, Comrade Stern," he said, trying to give his voice a tone of authority. "Your orders are to watch this pass, right?"

"That's right."

"Well, in that case, go on with what you were doing. We're going to go on our way."

The corporal hesitated and looked back at the seven soldiers accompanying him, who were prudently keeping a few yards back."Excuse me, Comrade Lieutenant, but I can't allow any of you to leave," he said, waving at the peculiar gaggle of followers.

"Who's your superior, corporal?"

"Commander Steimer."

"Steimer is General Walter's right-hand man," Jack whispered in his ear. "Bad business."

Alex nodded."We're leaving," he said. He glanced toward the east, where the first rays of the sun were beginning to appear. "We have no time to lose. I'll inform your commander personally." Waving his arm, he signaled to the procession that they were to keep moving.

Stern moved to stand in his way, crossing his rifle in front of him."Comrade Lieutenant, please," he said. "Don't make things more difficult for me."

Riley took a step forward until his nose was practically touching the Austrian's."Move over, Stern," he muttered under his breath. "I won't say it again."

The corporal, instead of cowering, took a step back and aimed his weapon at Riley. The soldiers with him did the same, raising their rifles to their shoulders and aiming at the two friends. "I have orders," the Austrian said to justify himself.

"Orders? What kind of orders?"

"To keep you here."

"Hang on… how?" Jack cut in. "Nobody knew we were coming. *Carallo*! We didn't even know ourselves!"

Stern did not answer this question.

"Whose orders?" Riley asked.

The Austrian took another step back without lowering his rifle, but kept his mouth shut.

"Whose orders?" Riley roared.

"My orders," someone answered from the darkness.

If someone had pierced them at that moment, not a drop of blood would have fallen to the ground. They were so taken aback they could not even articulate a coherent word as they saw André Marty come toward them with an air of satisfaction and a smile which seemed to grow wider by the moment.

"Well, well, well," he said, coming to stand in front of them with his hands behind his back. "'Ow good to meet again, *n'est-ce pas?*"

At last Jack was able to string together a few words that made sense. "How did you know…?"

The Frenchman waved a hand lazily. "Oh, it was nozing. I was sure you would try somezing, so I gave orders to the guards so zey would let you escape if you tried. Zen I just 'ad to set up a few patrols on the road and wait for you to appear, as you finally 'ave."

"But… but why?" Jack insisted. "I don't understand. We were already under arrest!"

"*C'est vrai*," he said with a nod. "But only for indiscipline and contempt, and in ze midst of an offensive like zis, you would surely not have been under arrest even for two days. I wanted to show zat you are traitors and punish you as you really deserve. I wanted… I want" – he corrected himself – "to set an example."

"You want to shoot us," Riley summed up.

Marty did not admit it, but the gleam in his eyes showed that it was exactly what he had in mind. Then, like a slaver inspecting the product on offer, he went past them to the group of civilians, who in turn were watching him with growing fear. "I see you brought wiz you a bunch of friends…" Pointing to them he exclaimed, "*Mon Dieu*! You even went to get ze nuns of ze village! 'Oo else did you bring?" He took one of Eustaquio's cousins by the arm. "Ze priest? Ze Secretary of ze Falange? Ze general of ze legion?"

"They are innocent civilians," Riley said, without much hope. "Refugees."

Marty gave a scornful laugh. "Innocent? Zere are no innocents in zis war! If zey were in Belchite and did not rise up in arms against fascism, for me zey too are accomplices of ze fascists."

"They're just nuns and farmers, not guerillas."

"Traitors," Marty replied. "Cowards."

"They haven't—"

"Silence!" he shouted. "You don't understand, do you? We won't win zis war if ze people don't rebel against oppression and fascism!" He shook the farmer's arm as if he were a rag doll. "It's for zem zat we fight! For zem! And 'ow do zey sank us? Running like rabbits! Zey must rebel! Fight in the trenches wiz zeir proletarian comrades! Die for ze cause if need be!"

"And you, Marty?" Riley asked. "Have you fought in the trenches? I don't remember ever seeing you wielding a rifle."

Corporal Stern and the other Thaelmann soldiers were following the conversation with particular interest. This made Marty answer Riley, although with obvious distaste."Comrade Stalin designated me personally as a political commissioner for ze party in ze Republican Army. It is a great responsibility which I cannot renounce, no matter 'ow much I might wish to fight in ze trenches."

"Sure... it's easier to shoot soldiers on your own side. What did you say they called him, Jack?"

"The Butcher of Albacete."

"Ah, yes. That's true. How many Republican soldiers did you have shot there, comrade commissioner? A thousand? Two thousand? Three thousand maybe?"

Even in the faint light of dawn they could see the Frenchman's face reddening."Stop zis chatter," he muttered under his breath as he pulled out his gun. "You!" he barked at his soldiers, pointing at Alex and Jack. "Take zeir weapons and take zem away, and zen shoot zem!"

Corporal Stern hesitated.

"Didn't you 'ear me, corporal?"

The Austrian swallowed with difficulty. "Comrade commissioner, instead of shooting them, shouldn't we take them to the general first, so he can decide what to—"

Marty covered the few yards that separated him from the corporal. Before he could finish the sentence, and without a word, Marty drew his pistol and struck him brutally on the temple with the butt. He was still holding his weapon as a warning when Stern's unconscious body fell limply to the ground and a thin thread of blood soaked the earth beneath his head.

Everyone watching, including the soldiers, reacted with suppressed repulsion to this unprovoked aggression on the part of the Frenchman.

"Anybody else want to discuss my orders?" he asked, looking around with the gun in his hand.

For a brief instant the soldiers seemed to hesitate about obeying this bully, but in the end fear took charge. With bent heads, two of them went over to Alex and Jack with the intention of disarming them, while the rest continued to aim their Mausers at them.

The two friends exchanged a fleeting glance, then drew their guns in unison. Jack aimed his at the two soldiers, while Riley, to everyone's surprise, threw himself at the political commissioner. Before Marty had time to react, he found Alex's arm circling his neck from behind and the barrel of the Colt pressing against his temple.

His arrogance and his certainty of the fear he inspired in all those around him had been the thing which, paradoxically, had made André Marty incapable of imagining such a daring feat. Even then, already a hostage, he still could not understand what was happening to him. He was the

"Butcher of Albacete". He was the one who inspired terror in others. It was inconceivable that he could be the victim at that moment. It was not possible... and yet here it was happening.

"Drop your weapons!" Riley ordered the soldiers. "Or I'll kill him right here and now!"

In astonishment they stared at Marty, who was barely able to breathe in the grip of Alex's arm. "You can't... kill me..." he mumbled with difficulty, eyes popping with asphyxia and fear.

"You don't think so?" Alex whispered, barely containing his rage. "Check this." He pressed his arm against Marty's neck even harder, until the commissioner began to kick and move his arms in spasms.

"Please..." he whispered, almost breathlessly.

Riley reduced the tension and let him gulp in air once again. "Order them to drop their weapons," he repeated. "Now!"

Marty, terrified, gestured to the soldiers to obey Riley. "Do... what... he says..."

Next, his gun still aiming at them, Jack made them sit on the ground on their own hands. "Take it easy," he said. "You can allege in your defense that you only did what the commissioner told you to. So don't do anything stupid. Okay?"

The seven soldiers nodded unhesitatingly. They were delighted to see Marty being given a dose of his own medicine.

Jack looked at the column of refugees, in whose faces fear and expectation were equally mixed, then at Marty, choked from lack of air and panic, and finally at the red sun, already rising above the horizon as if soaked in blood."What now?" he asked.

"Now it's our turn to wait."

He frowned in puzzlement."Wait? What for?"

Alex nodded toward the path that led to the Republican positions."For them to arrive," he said.

In the distance, a growing cloud of dust revealed the presence of a vehicle coming toward them. It was a military automobile bearing the flag of the International Brigades and the four stars of a general, fluttering in the wind.

22

Less than a minute later, the olive-green Citröen Traction Avant stopped with a screech amid a dense cloud of yellow dust. The flag with the four stars reserved for generals, which was also the symbol of the International Brigades, left no doubt as to who was riding in the car. Therefore, Alex was a little taken aback when the passenger door opened and a rather gangly man with ruffled black hair and thick brows that joined above the bridge of his nose jumped out. The man, who must have been twenty-five or so, carried a large camera slung round his neck. He put this to his face immediately and started taking photos of everything around him.

The next to get out was Commander Merriman. He looked around unsmilingly, fixed his gaze on Jack, who was still pointing his gun at the captive soldiers, then on Riley.

Riley let go of Marty at once and moved the Colt away from his head. "Lower your gun, Jack," he said to his friend, who realized the futility of his gesture and did so at once.

Last, as was to be expected, the shaven head and stern face of General Walter appeared at the door, watching everything with his severe, uncompromising air. He kept the door open, then with a gesture tinged with courtesy invited the last passenger to step out of the vehicle.

With her beret firmly set at an angle covering part of her blonde hair and that resolute air so typical of her, smiling confidently, Martha Gellhorn took the hand the general was offering her and stepped out of the car like a princess accompanying her consort.

The first thing that caught Walter's attention, obviously enough, was Sergeant Stern's unconscious body. He came to stand in front of him in silence, without troubling to check whether he was still alive. Next he turned to look at the soldiers, who were standing firm, albeit without their guns, still in a pile beside them. After this he noticed the forty or so civilians and nuns waiting expectantly at a prudent distance. Finally he swept his gaze over André Marty and the two men from the Lincoln wearing legionnaires' uniforms and with traces of black shoe polish still on their faces and hands. He then ordered two of the soldiers to carry Stern away, and crossed his arms meditatively.

In normal circumstances General Walter would grasp a situation at first glance, but on this particular occasion he felt himself incapable of imagining the events that might have led up to the scene in front of his eyes. He had no choice but to ask the Frenchman the inevitable question."What the hell is going on here, Marty?"

Like a beaten dog, Marty ran to the general, losing any trace of composure. He waved vehemently at Riley and Jack."Zey… zose two traitors, comrade general… zey tried to kill me," he stammered. Then, turning to the squadron, he shouted, "And as for you, you cowards, I'll deal wiz you later! Take zese two traitors and shoot zem *immediatement*! Zis is an order!"

The general put his hand on Marty's shoulder. "One moment, comrade commissioner," he said with frigid calm. "I will decide who gets shot and when."

Marty's reaction was halfway between surprise and indignation. "But…comrade general! Zey tried to kill me!"

"Is that true, soldiers?" the Polish general asked, addressing Jack and Riley.

They shook their heads. "It's not true, comrade general," Riley said.

"Not true, zey say!" Marty laughed nervously. "But zey are still holding zeir guns!"

"My gun is empty as you can see, comrade general," Riley went on, taking out the magazine and showing that it was empty. "And Sergeant Alcántara's is the same."

"Zat doesn't matter!" barked Marty. "Zey zreatened me!"

"With empty guns," Merriman noted from a discreet distance.

Marty glared venomously at him and turned his attention once again to Alex and Jack, then to the general. "Zese two soldiers disobeyed your direct order. You forbade zem to take anybody out of ze village, and now you see!" He waved triumphantly at the group of refugees with the restless photographer circling around it, taking photo after photo. "Zey've been hoodwinking you!"

The general glared severely at Riley. "That's true as well," he said in a distinctly threatening voice. "I don't like to be hoodwinked, lieutenant."

Alex cleared his throat. "My general…the truth is that we've done no such thing. You ordered me not to take civilians out of Belchite, and we haven't."

"What!! Zey didn't do it??" Marty exclaimed. "But zey are right here!" He ran to the group of civilians and stood in front of them, as if by doing this he was able to confirm that they were really there. "Zey are the proof of zeir insubordination!"

"I don't know these people, comrade general," Riley said, with his best poker face. "What about you?"

"Never seen them before in my life," Jack said shaking his head vigorously.

"Zey are lying!" yelled Marty. Seizing one of the novices violently by the neck, he forced her to look at the two men. "You! Say it!" he screamed in her ear, quite beside himself. "Say zey were ze ones 'oo brought you out of ze village!"

The novice burst into tears of fear, while the other sisters gave shrieks of terror.

"Say it, you damned *putaine!*" he roared, reaching for his gun. "Say you know zem!"

General Walter's deep voice rose above the uproar like the bray of an elephant. "Comrade Commissioner! What are you doing?" He was red with rage.

Marty looked up in surprise and realized that all eyes were on him, watching him with scorn and loathing. Even that annoying Hungarian photographer who had been with them for months like a horsefly did nothing but take photo after photo. "I… just meant for 'er to talk, comrade general," he muttered, with a parody of a reassuring smile. "You see, it's nozing…" He put his gun away and patted the nun's back. "It's nozing…" he repeated, letting the girl get away.

"Comrade commissioner…" the general repeated, shaking his head with evident disgust, "I'm very disappointed in you."

"Comrade general, please. I'm just trying to show you zat zese two men have committed insubordination and deserve to be punished. Zey disobeyed you!"

Walter turned his attention to Riley once again. "That's true," he agreed. "I gave you a direct order and you disobeyed it. That is a serious offense."

"Comrade general," Alex said putting his hand inside his shirt. "Let me show you something."

Walter's immediate reaction was to step back and reach for his own gun in a reflex movement, fearing Riley was going to draw a gun on him. But before he had time to take it out, he saw that it was nothing but a wrinkled sheet of yellowish paper.

"Here's what you asked me for, comrade general," Riley said handing it to him solemnly.

Walter stared at both sides of the smudged piece of paper, trying in vain to find some meaning in it. "What's this?" he asked at last.

Alex gave the trace of a triumphant smile. "What you ordered me to find out two days ago, comrade general. A plan of Belchite with all the enemy positions, quarters, artillery units and barricades. All I've done…" he added, standing to attention like a good soldier, "was follow your orders strictly."

General Walter carefully studied the basic map Riley had offered him, occasionally pointing out some unclear markings.

"And these?" he asked, with vivid interest. "Are they the artillery installations?"

"Mortars, comrade general. Here, and here."

"And these are barricades, right?"

"That's right. With nests of heavy machineguns."

The general passed his hand thoughtfully over his shaven skull."How did you manage to get such detailed information, lieutenant? Have you and the sergeant been over the entire village?"

"It wasn't necessary, comrade general." Alex patted the knife hanging from his belt and smiled mischievously. "A couple of legionnaires were delighted to cooperate, given a little encouragement."

A shadow of recognition appeared on the general's face, but he kept his attention on the drawing."Good… very good…" he muttered.

Martha Gellhorn, standing beside the general, winked at Riley.

He went up to her, took her by the arm and led her a few feet away."How did you find us?" he asked. "And how did you manage to convince the general to come? How—"

"Stop right there, sailor…" she interrupted him. "You wouldn't want a daring reporter to reveal her secrets, would you?"

"Cut the crap, Martha. How did you know where we were?"

"Javier, the kid you sent to our camp, spoke to Shaw and explained what you intended to do. Then he spoke to

Merriman, and he installed several watchmen to let him know by radio when they saw you coming. He came to talk to me and ask me to go with him to see the general."

"With you? Why?"

She smiled and, putting her hands under her breasts, lifted them provocatively."What do you think?"

"It can't be…"

"See for yourself. As they say here in Spain: two tits pull stronger than two carts."

"But, you and him?" He put his two forefingers together. "You know…"

Gellhorn opened her eyes wide and gave him an angry push."How can you think that?" she said with a grimace of disgust. "For God's sake, no. I flirted a little, that's true, but it was the promise of a great article that made him decide to come. It's all vanity, my dear," she finished, stroking his arm. "It's all vanity."

Riley nodded, in full agreement with that sentence."Well, whatever it was, thanks," he said solemnly. "You've saved my life and Jack's." He pointed to the refugees and added, "And possibly theirs too."

Gellhorn shook her head vigorously."No, Alex. You two have done that single-handed. Although… do you know what's going to happen to them?"

Riley shrugged."The problem was getting them out of the village, but at the moment they're just plain refugees, and a burden more than anything else. I'm hopeful Merriman will convince Walter that the best thing would be just to let them leave."

"I'm sure that's what will happen. But I'm concerned about what might happen to you and Jack."

He saw that Marty had gotten close to Merriman, Walter and Jack. However, instead of studying the map on the hood of the truck like the others, his attention was on Riley, whom he was watching with a look of hatred that foretold nothing good."We'll see. That map of the village with the rebel defensive positions and your promise of an article to the general might have saved our necks, but that bastard Marty has it in for us in the future, for sure."

"Well, you can worry about that when it happens," she said, taking his arm. "But now, and in exchange for saving your neck, as you say, you're going to tell me everything that happened tonight and give me an exclusive on your story. And not a word to Ernest. Do you understand me?"

"I'm all yours," he said smiling. "But I'm surprised not to see him here. Why didn't he want to come with you?"

"Oh, of course he wanted to. He almost had a fit when the general told him to stay in the camp. I convinced Merriman that with that impulsive character of his, he might complicate things even more and that it would be better if he didn't come."

"And why did you…?" Alex started to ask, but then he saw a roguish smile on the woman's face. "Oh… I see… the exclusive."

"All's fair in love, war and journalism." She smiled smugly.

At that moment Jack came toward them with an air of satisfaction."I think we've avoided the firing squad," he announced. "But my feeling is that we're not going to get off scot-free. We can't get out of being demoted to the ranks and arrested, in spite of that map of Belchite we brought back."

Riley shrugged stoically. "Well, okay. Taking into account how everything might've turned out, I think we can call ourselves happy with the result, wouldn't you agree?"

"Happy?" Jack repeated in astonishment. "*Carallo*, Alex, I still can't believe we're alive!"

Martha beckoned to the photographer. "Robert!" she called. "Stop taking pictures of the general and come here a moment. I want you to take a photo of these two brave men."

When he approached, she introduced them all. "Lieutenant Riley. Sergeant Alcantara, this is Robert Capa, one of the best war photographers in Europe right now."

"Only Europe?" he asked arching an eyebrow. Then he raised his camera and framed Martha standing in the center of the image flanked by Jack and Alex, each with an arm on her shoulder, like old friends. "Say *cheese*," he suggested while adjusting the lens, like one of the one-cent photographers in the Retiro Park.

The three were just opening their mouths obediently when there came a strident buzz over their heads. They raised their gaze in unison and saw a dozen twin-motor planes in attack formation, like sinister birds of ill omen, crossing the morning sky at three thousand feet in the direction of Belchite.

"The bombers…" Riley said in the ghost of a voice. "They're here already."

At that precise instant Robert Capa pressed the trigger of his Leica, immortalizing the two Lincoln Brigade members and the journalist with horror on their faces, seeing in advance the inferno that was about to break loose over that small village in no-man's-land.

Dedicated to the memory of the civilians and soldiers of both sides who died in the Battle of Belchite.

EPILOGUE

With the intention of easing the pressure of the army of rebels on the northern front and the siege of Madrid, during the last days of August 1937 almost twenty-four thousand men under the command of Generals Lister and Walter surrounded, bombed and finally attacked the small fortified village of Belchite, where about five thousand Franco combatants were concentrated.

The bombings by air and artillery began on August 26, and on September 1 an infantry attack was launched which turned into one of the bloodiest confrontations of the Civil War. The terrible fighting was carried out house by house, room by room. It went on until dawn of the sixth day, when the last three hundred rebel defenders, holed up in the town hall, attempted a desperate escape to Zaragoza from which only eighty of them came out alive.

The spear point of that attack was once again the decimated Lincoln Battalion which, as in the Battle of Jarama six months earlier, was used for political reasons as cannon fodder in the front line. In consequence they suffered the highest percentage of casualties of the whole Republican Army.

At the end of the battle, more than five thousand dead bodies carpeted the streets of Belchite and 2,411 rebel soldiers were taken prisoner by the Republican Army.

The final goal of the Republican offensive was really the city of Zaragoza, but the extraordinary defense of Belchite by Franco's troops delayed that offensive, and once the surprise factor was lost it could never be carried out. The final result of the Aragón offensive, planned by President Juan Negrín and the Minister of Defense, Indalecio Prieto, ended with a tactical Pyrrhic victory and a crushing strategic defeat.

Only six months later, on March 10th 1938, the insurrectionist army recaptured Belchite.

General Karol Waclaw "Walter" returned to the USSR after the end of the fighting, and served as a general in the Soviet Army until 1947, when he died in a skirmish with Ukrainian nationalists.

André Marty returned to France in 1939 and later settled in Moscow, fleeing from the scandal created by his cruel behavior in the Spanish Civil War. He died in 1956 without having been judged for his crimes.

Commander Robert Merriman never went back to teach at the University of California. When or where he died is unknown, as his body was never found, but a witness claimed to have seen him fall, fatally wounded, not far from Belchite, on April 2, 1938, during the retreat from Aragón.

Ernest Hemingway made him the protagonist of his novel *For Whom the Bell Tolls*, under the name of Robert Jordan.

Once the war ended, and after publishing *For Whom the Bell Tolls,* Ernest Hemingway married Martha Gellhorn to whom he had dedicated the novel and moved to Cuba. He covered the Second World War as a reporter, becoming so deeply involved that he ended up leading a group of partisans on the outskirts of Paris and came to be a front-line witness of the greatest battles of the war. On his return to the United States, he was awarded the Bronze Star for his courage in combat.

In 1945 Martha Gellhorn filed for divorce, and a year later Hemingway married Mary Welsh, who was to be his fourth and last wife. From then on his tendency to serious accidents and alcohol increased; in time this would bring about physical and mental deterioration as well as deep depression. He ended his life on July 2, 1961, shooting himself in the head with his favorite shotgun. In 1954, the author of *The Old Man and the Sea*, *Farewell to Arms* and *To Have and Have Not* had won the Nobel Prize for Literature.

Martha Gellhorn came to be regarded as one of the most important war correspondents of the twentieth century. As daring as Hemingway, or more so, she reported on the war from Finland, Hong Kong, Burma and Singapore, and even passed herself off as a stretcher-bearer so as to be present at the Normandy landings. Years later she also covered the conflict in Vietnam, the Six-Day War and the revolutions in Nicaragua and El Salvador. A traveler and a nomad, she considered as *living dead* those who never looked for new horizons for fear of being injured in the attempt. Her life's motto was *go to another country, another sky, another language, another setting.*

She has passed into history for having been married to Hemingway, but it is far more important to point out that she was a brave woman, free and intelligent, who took the reins of her own life and made an amazing adventure out of it.

On February 15, 1998, at the age of eighty-nine, suffering from cancer and nearly blind, she committed suicide by taking poison in her London home.

Thanks to Gellhorn's influence over General Walker, Eustaquio and his family, as well as the Dominican nuns, managed to reach their destination, as the general had agreed to supply them with transport to the outskirts of Zaragoza in exchange for an intended amorous encounter which never occurred.

Inevitably, Alex Riley and Joaquín Alcántara were reduced to the ranks and took part in the Battle of Belchite with the rest of their unit, standing out in the attack for their courage and devotion, even though André Marty took it upon himself to prevent them receiving any recognition for it.

The two friends went on fighting with the Lincoln Battalion until the Republican government disbanded the International Brigades and sent the few surviving volunteers back to their countries. Alex and Jack arrived in London at the beginning of 1939 with the intention of going from there back to the United States, from where they had set out almost three years earlier. But fate had a surprise in store for them. Not only would they not go back home, but they would inadvertently find themselves caught up in another adventure.

But that, of course, is another story.

OTHER TITLES FROM **FERNANDO GAMBOA**

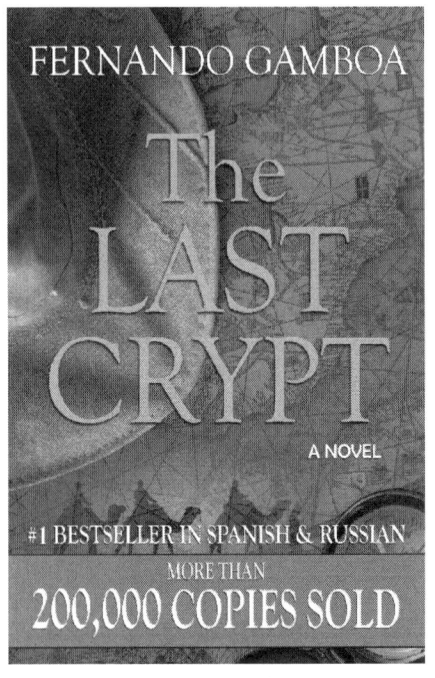

THE LAST CRYPT

Diver Ulysses Vidal finds a fourteenth-century bronze bell of Templar origin buried under a reef off the Honduras coast. It turns out it's been lying there for more than one century, prior to Christopher Columbus's discovery of America. Driven by curiosity and a sense of adventure, he begins the search for the legendary treasure of the Order of The Temple. Together with a medieval history professor and a daring Mexican archeologist they travel through Spain, the Mali desert, the Caribbean Sea and the Mexican jungle. They face innumerable riddles and dangers, but in the end this search will uncover a much more important mystery. A secret, kept hidden for centuries, which could transform the history of humankind, and the way we understand the universe.

BLACK CITY

An ancient mystery.
An impossible place.
An unimaginable adventure.

Professor Castillo's daughter has mysteriously disappeared in the Amazon jungle. Determined to find her, he begs Ulysses and Cassie to go with him. Unable to dissuade him and not wanting him to go on his own, they both accept to help their old friend in his crazy attempt at her rescue. The three embark on an incredible journey to a place which should not exist, the Lost City of Z
A journey nobody has ever returned from.

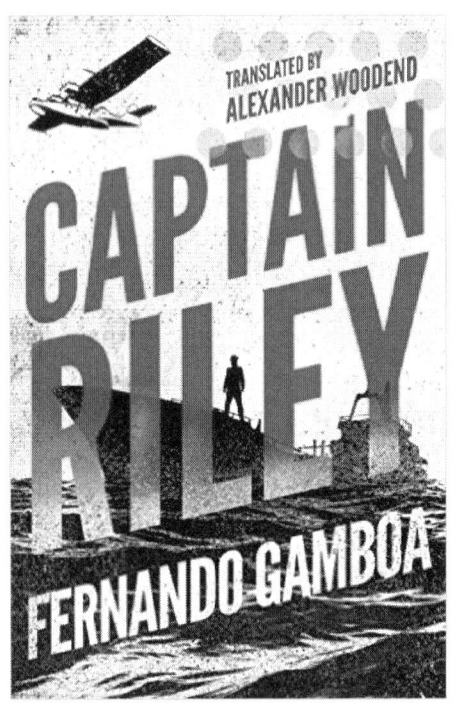

CAPTAIN RILEY

It's 1941, and Captain Alexander M. Riley and his crew of deep-sea treasure hunters believe they're setting off on yet another adventure—to find a mysterious artifact off the coast of Morocco for an enigmatic millionaire with questionable motives. Part-time smugglers, world travelers, and expats who have fought causes both valiant and doomed, Riley and his crew soon find themselves in the crosshairs of a deal much more dangerous than the one they bargained for. From Spain to Morocco to an Atlantic crossing that leads to Washington, DC, Captain Riley must sail his ship, the *Pingarrón*, straight through the eye of a ruthless squall and into a conspiracy that goes by the name Operation Apokalypse—a storm that only he and his crew can navigate.

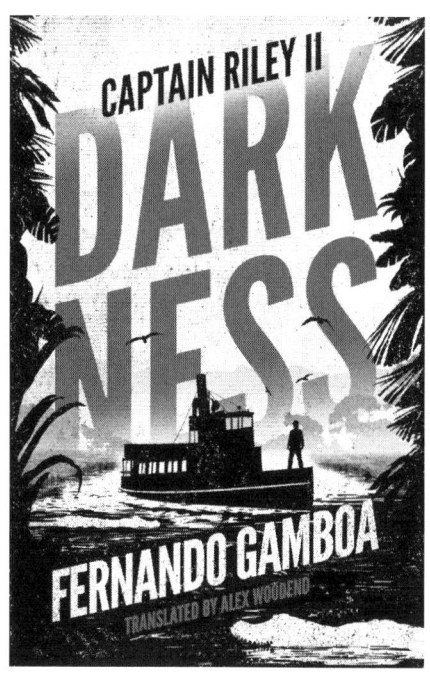

DARKNESS

From European shores to the heart of the African jungle, Captain Riley's *Pingarrón* embarks on new action-packed adventures.

On their last mission, Captain Riley, his loyal crew, and his girlfriend, Carmen, bravely averted a global disaster. Now, while World War II rages on, they hope that they are on more solid ground working for the US Navy. But when a job goes awry, the team finds itself taking a treacherous journey deep into the Belgian Congo. There, within the jungle, they will come face-to-face with wild animals, cannibals, and dark forces that shroud a decades-old mystery. They defeated the terrifying Operation Apokalypse that nearly destroyed them, but can they survive this?